1
Friedkin's Curse

Friedkin's Curse:

A Werewolf Tale of

Terror

By: Seth Tucker

Gracie,
Beware the moon!
-Seth Tucker

There is no one in the whole of humanity that I can think of who is more deserving of this book dedication than my beloved wife and best friend, Caralyn. She puts up with my insanity and crazy ways and agreed to do it until one of us is dead. That's worthy of a dedication: *To my dear, Caralyn.*

Prologue

The buck moved through the trees, occasionally stepping on a dry leaf and making it crunch as it made its way toward the edge of the water. The silver moon shone through the branches of the forest, casting a net of shadows. The lake reflected, the cold dead glow of the moon, as the Buck moved ever closer. It encroached upon the edge of the water and lowered its majestic head anointed with its crown of antlers toward the silver glow of the water. Quickly the Buck raised its head and stiffened. The muscles of its legs tensed as it prepared to gallop back into the sanctuary of the forest. The buck looked and listened scanning the woods for any threats. No longer sensing danger, the buck relaxed the corded muscles of his legs and lowered his head back to the water. Tentatively, the Buck drank refreshing its body with the cool, moonlit water.

From behind the Buck in the shadow-laced forest, two yellow eyes faintly glowed, marking the prey. Ears pricked up as they detected the sound of the deer drinking. Black claws flexed, trying to contain the rage that was building. The rage filled the beast, ever expanding like a balloon until the beast felt that it would explode. Then with a roar, the creature lunged out of the woods. The deer had its head halfway up from the water when the beast caught it. One of the thick, six-pronged antlers was snapped away as if it was a twig. The monster clutched deep into the fat around the Buck's neck with those fierce claws digging furrows in its flesh and covering the tan and white fur in crimson. With a fierce jerk, the deer's neck snapped, and its head was facing backwards. The beast dropped the body and howled into the night, and ripped into the warm meat

Friedkin's Curse

of the buck. Tearing muscle and cartilage, the fur clad nightmare fed on its victim.

After gorging itself, the beast looked into the water at the gore-coated visage staring back. With a mighty swipe, it destroyed the calm, mirrored surface and ran into the woods to satiate its hunger. Birds fled the trees in a mass exodus as the predator began the hunt again. Before the night was out, the beast had added a fox and a small nest of rabbits to its fare. Its hunger was satiated but could not be quenched by all the blood in the forest, soon it would seek a mate again, and it could feel another approaching. For now, it needed rest, so it slept and waited.

Part 1: School Days

The woods swallowed the small SUV. They had ventured out some 300 miles away to pick up Emera and Ameth's little sister, Ruby. The small town of Mead Hall was the last stop before entering the thirty-mile wooded area that housed the Friedkin School for Girls, a sprawling private boarding school. Ruby was smart enough to get accepted and her tuition was paid for by patrons of the school to help the girl get a better education. Jack, Emera's fiancé, watched as the Chevron gas station crossed the rear passenger window. He kept looking and the only thing he saw were trees. Emera sat beside him in the backseat while Ameth rode shotgun up front with her husband, Owen, driving the sport utility vehicle down the two-lane road. The world was washed a sickly green as the sun shone through the leaves that formed a canopy above the car. If it weren't for Ameth's iPod, there would not have been any music for the last hour; now the thump of the techno music seemed almost at odds with the green natural state of the woods.

As the trees began to blur, Jack felt almost hypnotized by the constant sea of green and brown before him. "Jack," Emera said shaking his shoulder. He awoke with a start, as the car exited the woods and emerged in front of a large brick building. "Here we are," Emera declared. She opened her door, and fresh air filled the car bringing with it the fresh smell of life from the forest.

Jack got out and leaned back to stretch out his cramped muscles but stopped in mid-stretch. He knew the school was big, but the giant four-story building that stood before him, looked like something out of a Harvard brochure. There were at least twenty -eight windows across the front, as well as a large porch, covered by an awning from the top of the building, which was supported by six columns. The steps leading to the giant oak double doors appeared to be solid granite. On the door were brass doorknobs and knockers suspended at eye level for Jack.

He was the tallest of the quartet, who had come to retrieve Ruby. At six feet three inches, he stood at least four inches taller than Owen and twice that over the sisters. By the way he carried himself, it was obvious that he had kept in shape but was starting to go soft, especially around the midsection. Still, it wasn't often that anyone tried to pick a fight with Jack. His dark hair, and tanned skin only complimented his physique.

Owen was of a smaller frame and his pale skin made it obvious that he had spent a great deal of time indoors. His black hair and goatee only made his pale skin more noticeable. Jack was the only member of the quartet to be making his first visit to the school. Owen had set up the school's new computer network, the previous summer, so the others approached the doors, while Jack admired the building

Ameth was the oldest of the three sisters, her brunette hair always cut short to keep her face framed, and set off her hazel eyes. Her slender shoulders blossomed into a full set of hips. She and Owen had been married for several years. Her demanding personality seemed to complement his meek demeanor.

Emera, the middle sister, had all the right curves in all the right places. Her eyes were the color of the ocean after a storm, and her head was topped off by a thick mane of raven black hair. In her quiet temperament was an iron reserve of strength that most people found comforting.

Ameth gave a whistle to Jack. "You coming?" She asked.

As Jack joined the group, Owen reached up and lifted the brass knocker. By the expression on his face, Jack assumed it was deceptively heavy. Owen raised the knocker and let go. It fell down with a loud thud. There was the sound of shuffling from the other side, and Jack almost expected a hunchbacked servant to open the door. He was relieved when the door was opened by a woman in her thirties, wearing a smart pants suit and her hair pulled back in a bun. She looked at them through her horn-rimmed glasses. "Can I help you?" She asked, not trying to cover the fact that she was in a hurry to get back to whatever she had been doing.

Owen stepped aside, and Emera and Ameth stepped up. "We're here for Ruby Divoe." Ameth said, flashing her best smile. "I believe we also had an overnight pass for two of your unused rooms."

"Just a moment please." The woman pushed the door closed, leaving the weary travelers to exchange confused glances.

Emera shivered as she thought about spending the night in the old building. Jack would have agreed it seemed like something out of a Victorian Gothic novel; even he felt a little uneasy about the place, although his bravado would never let him admit it. A minute later, the door was reopened by the same woman. "Please come in. I'm sorry about that, but I had to check with the headmistress before allowing guests. I'm Samantha Croul, I teach the sciences. Ruby is a pleasure to have in class." It sounded like a rehearsed statement.

Emera smiled and nodded. Ameth responded with a simple "thank you." Jack and Owen carried the bags in as the ladies followed Samantha.

Samantha's shoes echoed throughout the building as the three inch heel connected with the polished hardwood floors. The others in different types of athletic shoes made a few tiny squeaks that were lost in the echoing rumble of Samantha's steps. She led the way across the majestic

Friedkin's Curse

foyer decorated with paintings of very stern-looking, older people on the walls, and a row of phones set up in the back. The phones were the only newer piece of technology within sight. Samantha began to ascend a large, spiral staircase that wound its way to the three upper stories.

Emera and Ameth followed her as she began lecturing on the building and the school. Jack could not tell if Owen was paying attention or not, but Jack was lost in his own thoughts about the grand building. As they approached the second floor, Samantha explained that most of the classrooms were housed on this floor. Jack looked both ways down the hall and all he could see were double doors, comprised mainly of wood with small, porthole windows cut high in the door. The familiar glow of fluorescent light came through the porthole, and Jack could see lockers and the top corner of a cork board that he only assumed served to post bulletins.

Jack and Owen began sweating as they passed the second floor and headed toward the third; this, they learned, was where both faculty and students lived. Most of the married faculty lived in the nearby town, Mead's Hall, but someone had to stay with the children. Samantha, the headmistress, and another teacher by the name of Simone lived on the grounds year-round. Faculty quarters were to the right, while the students slept four to a room in two sets of bunk beds. The rooms off to the left were the ones reserved for students. *Just one more flight to go,* Jack thought as his arm began to burn from carrying his and Emera's bags. Owen was starting to breathe through his mouth, a sure sign that the weight of the bags was getting to him also.

Samantha led on toward the fourth and final floor, where apparently the guests' rooms were located. Emera and Ameth began losing pace with Samantha. Finally, at the top of the stairs, she turned toward them. "Well, ladies, your rooms are to the right, and gentlemen, yours are to the left. The bathrooms are at the far end of the respective halls, and you can have any room you choose, as you are our only guests at the moment." She smiled and started back down the stairs in a quick pace.

"Excuse me." Ameth said. "You mean my husband and I can't share a room."

Samantha stopped and turned back toward Ameth. "I'm sorry, I thought you knew they do not allow any mixed-sex cohabitation. That is also the reason why the married members of the faculty live in town."

"I know that when our parents came to pick up Ruby, they shared the same room." Emera interjected.

"I'm sure they did, but our new headmistress, Ms. Toews, instituted the rule this year. Since then, there have been no mixed gender rooms for visiting couples. I'm terribly sorry, but rules are rules."

Ameth began to open her mouth, when Owen waved a hand at Samantha. "Thank you, Ms. Croul. So, boys to the left, girls to the right."

Samantha's face lit up. "Yes, sir." She turned to head back downstairs but stopped. "Dinner will be served at six on the dot. If you care to join us, the dining room is on the first floor, just go through the double doors to the right once you leave the staircase." Her heels clicked her revelry as she gracefully flowed down the steps.

"This is crap, not letting us share rooms." Ameth protested.

Emera just shrugged. Owen smiled. "It's just for the one night; besides this way, you girls can talk about us all night and do each other's hair."

Emera smiled. "What are you boys going to do?"

Jack and Owen looked at each other, then back to the girls. "Make-overs!" They said in unison. All four of them laughed.

Jack and Owen walked the girls to the left hall double doors, where a white sign with bold red letters clearly read: NO GENTLEMEN BEYOND THIS POINT. There was a similar sign at the door to the other hallway warning off the ladies. Jack handed Emera the duffel bag that she had packed her stuff in while Owen shifted the bag around his shoulder to the front, unzipped it, and pulled out his articles. Then, he handed the bag to Ameth. "See you fellows for dinner?" Ameth asked.

Jack gave a quick nod and then started toward the hall, blowing Emera a kiss. "Wouldn't miss it." Owen said as he turned and followed Jack.

Ameth and Emera stopped at the first door on their left and turned the brass knob above an old-looking lock. The gears inside the handle made a few sounds of protest and then the door swung in with a high squeak. Ameth flinched at the sound. Emera walked past the door and looked into the small room. There were two wood frames where thin twin sized mattresses lay. In between the two frames was a small table, made of the same wood with a lamp sitting symmetrically in the center. There was a small rug at the foot of each bed, comprised of dark hues mostly. A window provided a small amount of sunlight to enter. The air was musty, and it was obvious that the rooms had not been aired out before their arrival. There was a click and a single halogen bulb snapped to life. Emera turned and saw Ameth standing beside a small light switch; mounted into the ceiling was one socket, and a halogen bulb was screwed into the socket, which cast a sickly white light around the room. Something on the wall moved, and Emera turned to see a floor length mirror mounted into the wall. She examined herself in the mirror, noticing the good fit of her jeans, and the way the blue shirt accented her eyes. She looked at her hair and felt frustrated; it was thick and hard to manage. She didn't feel like doing anything special with it for dinner, so she'd most likely put it back in a ponytail. Ruby would be so glad to see them. Last she had heard, their parents were going to come get her.

Ameth took out a small set of white sheets and began putting them on the bed on the left side of the room. Emera sat her duffel bag on the bed on the right, feeling momentarily nauseous, and stepping into the hall. Taking three deep breaths to ease, the nausea as it passed, the only thing that now remained was the tightness in her stomach where the muscles had begun to tighten. She brushed the dark locks out of her face and took several more deep breaths as she put her back against the wall. Ameth stepped out into the hall. "You okay?" She asked her younger sister.

Emera just nodded. "Yeah, it was too musty in there." She explained.

Ameth just turned and walked back into the room. Emera was not ready to go back into the room yet. She remembered her parents saying something about a look-out station on top of the roof and decided to go get Jack, and they would do a little exploring of the building. She leaned in the doorway to tell Ameth, but found her sleeping on the bed. Walking back through the double doors, she headed toward the men's hallway. She stopped at the doors and read the off-limits sign. She peeked around, did not see anyone and pushed through the doors. She heard sounds coming from the third door down and, made her way to the room where she found Owen sitting on the bed reading; he had changed into a pair of khakis and a polo shirt. Jack lay on his back still wearing carpenter jeans and a black t-shirt, looking aimlessly up at the pure white sheet rock of the ceiling. Emera cleared her throat, startling both men. Owen and Jack looked up. Owen returned to his book as soon as he realized who it was. "Dinner already?" Jack asked.

Friedkin's Curse

"No," she replied, shooting him a smile that revealed her perfectly straight teeth. "I thought maybe we could go exploring before dinner."

Jack hopped off of the bed. "Thought you'd never ask."

He made it to the door in three steps. "Owen, will you make sure Ameth is awake in enough time for dinner? We'll meet you down there." Emera told Owen which room they had chosen and then she and Jack went down the hall to the double doors.

They pushed through them and noticed a door set into the wall. It was directly between the two halls and was painted white; even the knob had been painted over. Jack looked at Emera, who only shrugged. Jack gave Emera a mischievous smile and headed toward the door. "What are you doing?" Emera asked. She was a little startled by how loud it sounded in the empty space and the echo also caught her off-guard.

"I'm exploring," Jack said as he pushed on the door.

When the door had been painted, the paint had formed a seal across the top of the frame, fastening the door securely. Jack reached into his front right hand pocket and pulled out a stainless steel pocket knife. Putting his thumb under the latch, he flipped out the three and a half inch blade. He glanced toward the stairs and placed the knife through the paint. "Maybe we shouldn't." Emera started.

"Too late now." Jack said smiling as he pushed the knife across the top of the door, cutting the thin seal the paint made.

The white door stuck, but Jack put his shoulder into it, and it opened with a small pop. Jack fumbled on the wall until he felt a familiar shape and pushed up on it. The room lit up with several antique light fixtures in the ceiling. Bulbs that were not as bright as the bulbs in the rooms flared to life. There were several small rows of wooden benches with backs, all stained a dark color. The floor appeared to have been stained the same color as the benches. Jack recognized the benches as church pews, and the small podium near the front stood before a cross. Jack squinted at the crucifix on the wall. There was something wrong with it but he could not tell what it was in this dim light. He jogged out of the room: "Emera, stay here; I'll be right back." He said as he headed back toward his and Owen's room.

Emera wished that he had not left her in the small chapel; something about it was off. Emera could not quite place how, but she could feel it. Something was wrong with this space. When Jack returned, he had a small metal cylinder only slightly larger than a pen. He pushed on the back end and three small LEDs came on giving much better light. Jack walked toward the crucifix on the wall and inspected the Christ figure hanging there. The emaciated body, and punctured side, hands and feet nailed in place. Jack was not looking at these things; it was the face that was off. He turned back to Emera. "Come take a look at this, please."

Emera made her way up beside Jack. At first glance, it did not look any different than every other crucifix she had seen. All the same, though, it gave her a very eerie feeling. She looked at Jack for some sign of what he had seen. He was looking at her intently. "The face," he whispered.

Emera and Jack turned back to the crucifix. Almost immediately, Emera saw what he had meant. The small golden face was twisted with what looked like rage, saliva frothing from his bared teeth. Looking closer, she noticed that all of his teeth were triangular, like fangs. She felt an overwhelming need to leave the room; there was something incredibly unholy about this chapel. She reached up and took Jack's arm. He looked at her. She was so uncomfortable she had started to shake. Jack took his attention off of the crucifix and wrapped an arm around her. "What's wrong?" He asked, genuine concern in his voice.

She looked up and focused on his eyes, those brown eyes which always showed so much compassion. She stared at them until she was confident that her voice would not quiver. "We shouldn't be here."

"I think you're right." Jack agreed.

He and Emera made their way back through the benches, never turning around to look at the crucifix. Jack turned off the light and closed the door. The foyer outside the door seemed warmer than the air inside the chapel had been. Jack broke the silent and oppressive air that had followed them through the door. "I understand why they don't want people going in there. A little bit creepy."

"Yeah, that face, it was so angry."

"Maybe it was the artist's idea of anguish." Jack offered, even though he had seen some inhuman rage portrayed on the small, plaster face. "Let's see what's down on the far end of your hall, shall we?" Jack asked, offering Emera his arm.

Emera curtsied and slipped her forearm through his. They began down the ladies' hall, keeping quiet as they passed the room where Ameth lie sleeping on the bed. They passed by the other closed doors with their brass knobs until they came to the end of the hall and were faced with a heavier door than the others and a different kind of knob. Jack turned the knob and opened the door, leaning through the door to see a large window set into the wall above a small landing and stairs leading up to the landing and from the landing to another door. Jack held Emera's hand as he cautiously tested the stairs. A few of them creaked, but they all held firmly. They reached the door, a newer, metal storm door with a deadbolt and a much newer-looking doorknob than most of the doors they had come across. He turned back the deadbolt, screeching loudly in the small space as it withdrew from the door frame into the door. Turning the knob, he opened the door and tested the outer knob; it did not turn. He flipped the small thumb switch on the interior knob and unlocked the outer knob. "That would have been bad," he said smiling to Emera.

She just nodded giving him a small smile, as they walked out onto a platform maybe twenty feet square with a roof over it. There was a metal support column in the middle and a post in each corner that held up the roof. Along the edge was a rail with the slats placed close enough together to prevent anyone from falling underneath. All around the school, the sun heading toward its western resting place bathed the treetops in its rays, casting a reddish glow over the canopy. *It looks almost like blood.* Emera thought, then shook her head, banishing such dreadful thoughts.

Jack wrapped his arms around her waist from behind and gave her a small squeeze. She leaned her head back against his shoulder, and he could smell the sweet scent of strawberries her shampoo always left. He kissed her on the temple, and she lifted her face up toward him. He leaned over her shoulder and kissed her again, feeling the soft fullness of her lips. They broke the kiss and returned to watching the sun's descent. The far edges of the forest toward the east were already dark. It almost sent a melancholy cloud into Jack's mind, but then the warmth of Emera pressed against him forced it away. The sun would rise again in the morning, and the world would be bright again.

Jack glanced at his watch. "Shoot." Emera broke the embrace, looking startled. "It's after six. We're late for dinner."

They spent more time than they realized in the chapel and then had both been so mesmerized by the view from the platform that time had slipped past them. They hurried down the stairs and back through the hallway. Walking at a quick pace, they passed Emera and Ameth's room, noticing that Ameth was not there. They came into the little foyer, and the chapel did not cross their mind. They descended the three flights of stairs so that when they reached the bottom floor, they were both breathing heavy. Across the grand room stood two large, white doors with gold accents; behind them came the sounds of conversation with an undertone of rattling silverware. Gripping the golden handle Jack opened the door and bowed letting Emera enter first.

Jack followed closely and closed the door behind him. They saw three rows of long tables, which could have easily sat sixty people per row but were nowhere near full, both with what appeared to be an entree and side items populating the centers as people sat on both sides of the tables. Toward the head of the table on the left sat an older woman with a stern face, whose glance showed nothing but disapproval for Emera and Jack's entrance. At the head of the other table was Samantha, her hair still in a bun. Sitting at the midpoint with her back to the wall was another woman who appeared to be older than Samantha, her hair a healthy chestnut color. Emera assumed this was Simone. She had a kind face, and her body language gave the impression that she was a quiet individual. "Emera!" Ruby shouted from across the giant dining room.

She rose from the headmistress' table where she had been sitting beside Ameth and Owen. Waving her arm, she signaled to the two seats across from her. The places had been set ahead of time. Her long, brunette hair had been put up in a French braid, which travelled down her spine to the center of her back. She was dressed in a school uniform that matched the other girls, a blue button up shirt and knee-length khaki shorts. Ruby seemed to be set aside by her reddish brown hair and light freckles that spotted her face, which was itself filled with excitement at seeing her other sister.

The headmistress turned her stern gaze from Emera to the youngest sister Ruby. Ruby gave no notice of the older woman's stare. Emera and Jack made their way down the wall until they came to the two seats that Ruby had indicated. Jack pulled Emera's chair out for her and scooted it under her as she sat before taking the seat beside her and taking a deep breath, inhaling all the wonderful smells of the meal. In the center of the table and the plates was a large roast, sitting on a silver charger. On both sides of it were mashed potatoes, carrots, and broccoli. Jack's mouth watered looking at all the food while Emera passed her plate getting a small helping of each item. Jack, however, drew the scorn of the headmistress again when he asked for an additional spoonful of potatoes. Ruby smiled at Jack. He simply nodded at her. "Don't you love my school, Jack?" Ruby asked.

"I do. It's very nice. I bet there's a lot of history here." He said smiling.

"Why don't you let our guests eat, Ruby?" Ms. Toews said, finally speaking. Ruby sat smiling at all four of them, silent for the rest of the meal.

They were served milk with their meal. Even the headmistress was drinking it. After the meal was finished and the children who had not gone home yet began to clear the tables, the headmistress rose from her seat, dressed in a pearl-buttoned blouse that came evenly to her neck and a floor-length skirt, her shoes barely visible from underneath. Jack thought she looked a century behind the times. Emera and Ameth would have associated her with the Wicked Stepmother from *Cinderella*. Owen was reminded of Ms. Gulch from *The Wizard of Oz* in the company of the headmistress.

Ms. Toews asked all the adults if they would like to go into the drawing room. She led the way with Samantha and Simone following closely behind her. The quartet, who had come to take Ruby home, also followed. Exiting the dining room, through a smaller set of double doors, these had a natural oak coloring, the headmistress led the adults across a hallway and into a room with several bookshelves, two old Victorian-style leather couches and five matching chairs. There was a fireplace set into the wall, but with the summer upon them there was no need for a fire. "Would you like some coffee?" The headmistress' voice was as prim and proper as her posture.

Emera did not like the headmistress; she seemed very cold. None of the group was overly drawn to her. Ameth assumed she was just a lonely woman who had dedicated her life to teaching. Owen had not thought much on it. The headmistress was just not a people person to him, which he didn't mind at all. But to Jack, she seemed like countless others he had met over the years. She was an older woman who at one time had been a younger woman who thought she was better than everybody else. From the scorn in her eyes and tone of her voice, she still felt that way.

Samantha and Simone stood waiting for their guests to respond to the headmistress. "Yes Ms. Toews. We'll both have some." Ameth said, smiling politely at the woman.

"I'd love some thank you." Emera said, being polite. Her traveling companions knew she didn't like coffee.

"No, thank you." Jack said, watching the cold green eyes of Ms. Toews, turn once more into that scornful glare he had seen through most of dinner.

"Ladies," the headmistress said, nodding to Samantha and Simone. They left the room, leaving the four guests with the headmistress. "I hope you had a pleasant trip. Ruby lives a few days travel away doesn't she?"

"Yes." Responded Owen as he and Ameth sat down in the nearest of the couches, the leather creaking underneath them. Emera sat on the end of the sofa while Jack took up the chair next to the sofa sitting across from the headmistress.

"I have met Mr. Owen and Ruby's lovely sisters, but I do not believe I have had the pleasure of making your acquaintance." She said, smiling at Jack.

Jack suppressed a shiver; that smile seemed foreign on her face. "Jack Houston." He stood up and extended his hand. She lightly shook it.

"Charmed," she said, but the feeling did not show in her eyes. Everyone in the room could feel the woman's churlish nature.

Jack sat back down, and Simone and Samantha returned, Simone carring a small tray with a crystal bowl containing sugar and a small pitcher with cream, while Samantha carried a large, silver coffee pot on her tray with six cups all containing the blue and white design found most commonly on Dutch merchandise. Jack sat smelling the aroma of the coffee. It was very strong; Jack assumed they must make the coffee fresh from the beans in the kitchen.

After almost a half hour of sitting around making small talk, predominantly about Ruby, the two couples excused themselves to go to their rooms for the evening. As they left, the three faculty members remained to finish their coffee. The children were already in their rooms, reading or talking amongst themselves, Jack assumed. There were no televisions on campus. Maybe some of them had radios.

As they approached the foot of the steps, the group was discussing the meal they had just enjoyed when Emera cut them short. "Did you hear that?" She asked.

"I thought I imagined it." Ameth said, confirming that there had been some noise.

"What were we supposed to hear?" Owen inquired with a smile on his face.

"It sounded like a. . ." Ameth paused, looking at Emera for assistance.

"Scream?" Emera ventured with Ameth nodding her agreement.

"I didn't." Jack answered as Owen nodded his head.

The group began their way up the stairs. A window-rattling howl erupted as they reached the second-floor landing. It sounded like it came from inside, but that was not possible. From the third floor came the thunderous sounds of running feet. The students came running from their rooms, fear splashed across their faces. They were all now in their pajamas. The headmistress and the teachers were at the very foot of the stairs as the children came running past the guests on the second-floor landing and rushed down to the people they knew. Only Ruby stayed on the second floor, cowering behind her sisters. Jack looked down the stairs and realized by the look on their faces that everyone thought the howl came from inside.

The scorn in the headmistress' eyes had been replaced with shock and a small twinge of fear. Jack cleared his throat. "Did anyone see anything?" He asked, speaking loudly enough for all the people at the foot of the stairs to hear him. The adults looked around as the students shook their heads.

"No," responded the headmistress.

Ruby pulled on Jack's hand. Jack kneeled in front of her, and Owen leaned over to listen to her. "Jasmine saw a monster climbing up the side." Jack listened very intently. "The headmistress thought we made it up, but we didn't. I saw it two days ago standing in the woods."

Jack patted Ruby on the shoulder. She was a child, but she wasn't prone to lying or flights of imagination. "Okay, everyone stay down here. Owen and I are going to go upstairs and make sure that nothing is here." Emera and Ameth looked at the men in protest. "Downstairs with everyone else. Get them in a nice warm room, and we'll be down soon." Jack said comfortingly.

"Promise?" Ruby asked as she slipped one of her hands into Emera's grasp and the other hand into Ameth's.

"Absolutely." Owen said smiling.

"Cross my heart." Jack added, marking an X over his heart with his index finger.

Ruby nodded and started pulling at her sisters. The men turned to start up the next flight of stairs when Ruby called from behind them. "It came from above us." Jack nodded.

Owen and Jack took the far railing and made their way up slowly, trying to get the best vantage point for the next section of stairs as they made their way. The headmistress gathered everyone else into the auditorium, while Samantha went to make cocoa for everyone.

"A monster?" Owen mused barely above a whisper. "I wonder what it really is."

"I don't know, but whatever it is, they think it climbed up the side of the building." Jack responded. As they approached the landing to the fourth floor, Jack stopped abruptly and Owen followed suit, nearly bumping into him. "Owen, I brought my .38, so let's swing by the room and pick that up, just in case." Jack whispered, never taking his eyes off of the fourth floor landing.

"Why'd you bring it?"

"I don't like going on long trips without it, besides we may need it."

"What are we going to need it for?"

Jack motioned Owen up beside him. "When we came down for dinner, that door was closed." Jack pointed to the chapel door, which they had closed on their way out. It stood wide open and from inside came the sounds of something shuffling around. "So let's assume it didn't climb the wall; how'd it open the door then? On three, we make a run for the room." Owen nodded, his mouth going dry as he realized they may actually find something. Jack was just as nervous, his stomach fluttering and palms sweaty.

"One."

"Two."

"Three!" Jack yelled, and they both broke for the hallway with their room. Both of them sprinted all out, keeping stride with each other. Owen was first through the door, and Jack was right on his heels. Turning back and putting his shoulder into the door, Jack slammed it shut and braced himself against it.

"Did it come after us?" Owen said, doubling over panting.

Jack trying to catch his breath as well took a few seconds to respond. Finally, he was able to speak. "I don't think so, but just in case, come lean against the door."

Owen took Jack's place. Jack pulled his duffel bag up from the floor and sat it on his bunk. He reached straight through to the bottom and pulled out a small, leather zip-up case. He opened it to reveal the soft fabric inside where lay a Smith & Wesson .38 Special. It had a six-inch, stainless steel barrel, leading from the sights to the hammer where the black pistol grips took over. Also in the case was a box containing thirty bullets. He took out the pistol, pushed open the cylinder and loaded it. Taking the box of ammunition, he pushed it into the side pocket of his jeans near his knee. He also removed his knife and handed it to Owen.

Jack's dad had been a policeman for thirty years. He always made sure his son knew how to handle a weapon. Now holding his dad's old service revolver, Jack felt calm. Trusting in his dad's good luck to help him.

With the gun pointed at the ceiling, Jack began to explain his idea. "You open the door, and I'll sweep the hall, then we'll make our way to that door." Jack reached in his back pocket and pulled out his flashlight. He clicked it on made sure it worked and then turned it off.

"Now or never," Owen said gripping the doorknob, ready for the intruder to spring at it from the other side.

Jack steadied himself and took in a deep breath. He nodded to Owen, who pulled the door open wide. Jack leveled the gun at the empty doorway. Taking three quick steps he leaned out the door sweeping from the hallway entrance to the far end. He exhaled and raised the gun toward the ceiling once more. "Okay," he said to Owen.

Owen stepped out into the hallway. From the other side of the entrance doors, came a clicking sound with a steady rhythm to it. As Jack and Owen moved closer to the doors, the clicking grew louder. "Something's coming." Owen said, putting his hand on Jack's shoulder.

The clicking stopped. Something was blocking part of the light from under the door. The door began slowing inching open. Black obsidian claws with gore -encrusted tips made their way through the door

29
Friedkin's Curse

attached to a charcoal gray fur-covered hand, that was eerily human and yet far too jointed and animalistic. Next in sight was a face unlike anything either man had ever seen outside of a movie or their worst nightmares. Owen's knees buckled and he slumped to the floor. Jack stood with his mouth gaping as the creature's lips pulled back to reveal its strong jaws, dripping with saliva and filled with teeth yellowed and bloodstained. The lips and muzzle of the beast were matted with blood and gore. From deep within the throat of the beast came a growl and the one hand they could see gripped for purchase preparing to spring. Owen fought for words in his throat and finally found one.

"Shoot."

Jack was shaken out of his fear by the simple realization that he still had the pistol. He aimed and fired. He had not taken the proper time to aim, but the bullet still struck the meat of the beast's shoulder. The door closed as Jack saw the beast stand up and peer through the windows cut into the doors. It glared at him, with yellow eyes full of hate and hunger. Blood poured from the wound in its shoulder as it snarled and turned. Jack grabbed Owen by the shoulder and pulled him to his feet. "Come on." They made it through the doors in time to see the beast run and at the last minute drop to all fours and leap from the top of the fourth floor stairs to the landing on the floor below.

The doors to the lady's hall blew open; both Owen and Jack saw the door standing open at the far end of the hall, the same door Jack and Emera had come in from after their sojourn on the lookout perch. "Go close that door and make sure it's locked." Jack said pointing down the hall and handing Owen his flashlight. "I'm going after it."

Owen took the flashlight and ran down the hall. Jack took the stairs, slowly. Both he and Owen had seen how far it could jump and he did not want to be pounced on by the monstrosity. As he came into view of the landing, he saw the thing kneeling on its haunches in the corner of the landing. It seemed to be grunting. Finally, it threw something behind it and turned toward Jack. Taking aim this time, Jack began putting pressure on the trigger, but the beast leapt off the stairs and landed onto the foyer floor. Jack watched as it hit, cracking the wood-finished floor beneath it. When it looked up at him – a surprise in itself for something seemingly so bestial - Jack would have sworn it grinned at him. "Jack!" Owen called from the top of the stairs.

"It's on the main floor." Jack yelled, sprinting down the stairs, caution abandoned as the threat to Emera, Ameth, Ruby, and the others settled into his mind. He could see it heading toward the dining hall and crouched to fire again, this time missing but only barely. The beast stumbled, afraid of being hit again. "Ladies, stay where you are! Everything's all right!" Jack bellowed, hoping that everyone could hear him.

From the other side of the dining hall came a great clattering sound, exiting the dining hall, Jack came upon the kitchen. It was white tiled with steel racks loaded with utensils. There was a swinging door on the other side of the room, and it was moving as if something had ran through it in a hurry. Dashing past the steel racks, Jack slowed down as he came around the last rack, which housed a wide variety of cutlery and electronic cooking utensils. Stepping over a tray containing a large, shattered pitcher of what appeared to be cocoa, he gave the door a strong kick to send it swinging viciously into the hallway. Satisfied that nothing was waiting on the other side of the swinging door, he heard another door knocking. He exited the swinging door as Owen came around the last steel rack. The door at the end of the hallway stood open, revealing the woods and darkness. A storm was blowing in, and the wind kept the door knocking against the hall wall. There were several other doors, leading off of the hallway. Most of them were locked, all except for one that had a wooden stairway leading down into a rock-walled hallway. Jack assumed it was some sort of pantry.

Approaching the exterior door, he grasped the back of it, causing the knocking to stop. Looking down, he noticed three rock steps leading to the ground. On the second step was a small spattering of blood. Jack pulled the door to and locked it. He turned to Owen. "See anything interesting?"

"Looks like some claw marks and something definitely climbed up on the roof out there. Some of the shingles are shredded." Owen said. "What was that?"

Jack looked out through the window and noticed for the first time that there were thick iron bars across the glass. Thinking about it, almost all the windows seemed to have that same black, wrought iron across all the windows. Jack filed that away for later and brought his mind back to Owen's question. "I don't know. Let's just hope we can get out of here in the morning and not run into it again. For now, we should find everybody. They've got to be terrified."

Owen folded the knife and handed it back to Jack. The two men went down the hall, opening all the unlocked doors they came to. They found everyone huddled into the auditorium. It was a spacious performance hall with a large stage on the far end and rows of wooden chairs where the seat flipped up when no one was in them. It could easily accommodate two-hundred guests. Everyone was sitting in the chairs half-turned toward the door. Conversation was sparse, but the sounds of the small voices filled the large auditorium. When the door opened, Owen and

Jack heard a hush fall on them. "It's okay, it's just us." Owen said, opening the door to expose himself and Jack.

Everyone let out the breath that they had held. Ameth and Emera got up and ran to their men. "What was it?" Asked Ameth.

Owen and Jack exchanged glances. "Well, we can't say for sure. It was pretty quick, wasn't it, Jack?" Owen asked, giving Jack a cautious look.

Jack nodded. "But it's gone, and I don't think it'll be back tonight."

Jack finished speaking and noticed everyone looking at his hand; he followed their gaze and saw that they were staring at the pistol. He quickly put it under his belt in the back of his jeans.

"Is that what we heard?" Ms. Toews inquired.

"Partly, your intruder was rather noisy himself. If I were you, I'd have the police or animal control come out here in the morning." Jack's eyes met Ms. Toews. She seemed nervous.

"I will call the local constabulary first thing in the morning." Ms. Toews suddenly perked up and looked at Jack and Owen. "Did you see Samantha?"

Owen and Jack shook their heads in unison. "Where was she?" Owen asked.

"She was in the kitchen, making cocoa for the children." Simone responded.

"She wasn't there when we went through." Jack said reaching back for the revolver; his mind flickered to the shattered pitcher of cocoa.

Turning to go back into the house and search for the missing teacher, Jack jumped slightly as she came around the door frame. She had some dirt smudges on her face, her hair which had been neatly pulled back at dinner was now disheveled with small tendrils of her sandy brown hair dangling free, her clothes were dirty and with a few small cuts on them, and blood was flowing down her hand from inside her torn jacket sleeve. Jack reached for her, but she held up her hand for him to stop. "I'm fine. When I heard something enter the dining room, I ran and hid in the cellar." She explained.

"What happened to your arm?" Ameth asked, pointing to the blood.

"I fell backwards while I was coming back upstairs." She responded. Simone walked past them, carrying a small, white, plastic container; she opened it, and everyone saw the red cross indicating a first aid kit. Samantha pulled back her ripped shirt sleeve, revealing a gash running the length of her forearm. It was an ugly wound, ragged, and swollen around the edges. She saw everyone looking at her and smiled weakly. "There seems to be a nail sticking out of the wood, and it caught me."

Having removed his hand from the revolver as soon as Samantha had come into the room, Jack stepped aside and ushered Samantha onto one of the nearby seats. Simone stayed with her, applying an antibiotic cream and bandages. Jack turned to go back toward the kitchen, and Emera followed him. Owen stayed in the room with his arms wrapped around Ameth. Emera heard one of the little girls ask if they should go back to their rooms. She could not hear Ms. Toews response, but judging by the shambling feet leaving the auditorium, she could surmise that they had been sent back to bed. Emera followed Jack as he walked down the hall and turned to head into one of the doorways. He saw Emera out of the corner of his eye and turned to look at her. She smiled and he smiled back. "What do you think you are doing?"

"Following you." She said, pushing a lock of black hair out of her face with her index finger.

"Okay," he said, waving her up to him. She walked quickly to his side as a draft wafted up from the doorway. "I'm assuming this is the cellar. Thought it might come in handy to know the layout, just in case."

The stairs were wooden and did not look safe to walk on, but they held Jack and Emera without so much as a protesting creak. The walls were made of stone, as was the floor. As they descended the steps, the air grew cooler and ta pungent scent laced the air, very earthy and musty. The rock wall that Jack and Emera were using as a guide down the stairs grew cold and damp the closer they got to the stone floor beneath. Stepping from the wood to the stone floor, Jack and Emera saw small halogen lights hanging unshielded from the ceiling. Jack saw only four lights, and the dark stone floor and stone walls seemed to swallow what little light they put off. Slowly, Jack eased away from the stairs, Emera directly behind him. Looking down into the murk of the corridor, Jack could not discern any type of opening in the walls. Apparently, it just led back to another wall. Jack kept his eyes open for any sign of blood, since there was not any on the stairs, and he never saw any in the corridor.

Jack walked the corridor with Emera, and as they neared the end, it became apparent that it was not another wall, but a door. It was old and strong, made of what Jack could only surmise was iron or steel. It seemed sturdy, and there was a place for a rope or chain to keep the door sealed, but it was empty. Set near the top of the door was a small opening with three bars covering it. Jack peered through but could not see anything beyond the glow of the last halogen light. He reached into his back pocket but remembered when he found it empty that he had given Owen his flashlight. The pungent odor came from the other side of the door, and while Jack was looking through the slotted opening, a wave of it swept into his face, gagging him.

Emera was silent, looking around the dark hallway toward the stairs they had come from when she saw something reflect a little bit of the light. "What's behind the door?" Emera whispered, not prepared to hear the echo of her voice off of those dark walls. She wondered if her voice would be swallowed by the walls like the light was.

"I can't say for sure, but I think it may be an old root cellar." Jack turned and looked back the way they came, then turned back to the door and looked at the ceiling on the other side of the metal door. "This goes out beyond the house." He said to himself.

"What?"

"The ceiling is dirt; if this was under the house, we'd be able to see the foundation." Jack turned back toward Emera. "You ready to get out of here?"

"You bet; it's cold and drafty and this place scares me." Her voice was still only barely above a whisper.

They walked back toward the stairs, and Emera bent down and reached under the first stair. Jack tilted his head to the side in puzzlement. She removed something shiny from underneath the stair and held it out so he could see it. It was a silver wolf head on a thicker silver chain. The wolf appeared to be snarling, but with the poor lighting in the cellar, it was hard to tell. Emera looked at it and then asked. "Do you think Samantha dropped it?"

Jack shrugged his shoulders. The two end links on the chain looked like they been broken.. "You can ask her." He suggested.

Emera slipped the pendant and chain into her pocket and began ascending the steps. Jack turned around and took one last look down the corridor to the door on the far end. He was getting the feeling that he was being watched. The hairs on the back of his neck stood on end for a minute and then the sensation passed. He shook it off and climbed up after Emera.

Ms. Toews was waiting in the study doorway as Jack and Emera came by. "Excuse me," she said, placing her hand on Jack's forearm. Her skin was cold and felt rough. "Might I have a word with you?"

Emera looked at Jack, who nodded, and they found themselves seated on the sofa as Ms. Toews seated herself across from them. "What was this place built for?" Jack asked.

Ms. Toews showed obvious surprise at the question. "It was built to be a home for General Milford Friedkin, shortly after he left the Union Army in 1866."

"Then why all the iron bars and thick doors?" Jack asked as Emera was looking at the study windows, noticing the thick black bars running across them.

"I assure you, I don't know why the house was built the way it was." She said with a look of curiosity on her face. "What did you really see? The children are not here now, and I feel it imperative for me to know the entire truth before I summon the local authorities."

"I don't know." Jack said, looking into the back of the fireplace. "I've never seen anything like it before. It fits the description Ruby gave me though. She said that they've told you about it before."

"We have had the girls swapping ghost stories now that their studies are over, giving each other a case of overactive imagination." She shook her head, dismissing the idea.

"Well, I'd pay a little more attention to them. Because if they have been seeing it, that means it's in the area." Jack stood up and walked to the door. "Ms. Toews, it was in the chapel."

"What chapel?" She asked.

"The one in the foyer of the fourth floor." Jack said.

"What was it doing in there?" She asked.

Jack shrugged. "I'm going to take a look right now. You are welcome to join me."

Jack, Emera, and Ms. Toews climbed the stairs. Jack and Emera walked slowly allowing the older woman to keep up. When they came to the third-floor landing, Jack ushered the women on ahead of him as he kneeled to inspect the object the creature had thrown. It sat in a congealing pile of blood. He opened his pocket knife and prodded the object. It moved, and Jack could see its slightly deformed tip. Standing on end, the bullet was a lead hill in a field of red. Jack rose quickly and went up the stairs to the ladies.

Ms. Toews stood by the chapel door, while Emera stood by the head of the stairs. As Jack came up, Emera turned to him. "What was it?" She asked.

He leaned in close as if to place a kiss on her cheek and whispered; "the bullet." Her eyes opened wide in amazement. Jack made a small shushing noise, left the stairs, and went to the chapel doorway. "Well?" He asked Ms. Toews.

"I was waiting on an escort. Ms. Divoe refuses to enter." Jack looked back at Emera, who only shook her head. Ms. Toews reached her hand in the door and flipped the switch, turning on two overhead lights that did little to illuminate the area.

Jack went in first with Ms. Toews close behind him. The air was no longer musty but now a wet pungent smell like a butcher shop hung in the small space. Under the crucifix with the snarling Jesus was a small bundle sitting on a black cloth. Jack could not quite make it out, but when he moved closer, he found the source of the smell. A raccoon had been slaughtered, its back broken. The only pieces that remained were the bones and some flesh on the hind and fore quarters. The entire abdomen and chest and been torn out and the black cloth was actually the animal's congealing blood. Ms. Toews gasped and fled the room. Jack checked along the wall to make sure that everything else was as it should be. He noticed that there were deep scratch marks in the bottom of the podium located in the direct center of the room.

Covering his nose and mouth to dampen the smell, Jack turned and left the room, too. As he exited, he turned off the lights and closed the door behind him. Ms. Toews stood by the stairs, not looking back toward the chapel door. "Mr. Huston, I must agree with your earlier recommendation that we contact local law enforcement. They will be here in the morning." Her head gave a curt nod, and she began her descent down the stairs. "Have a pleasant sleep."

Emera scoffed. "Easier said than done."

"Get your stuff. You and Ameth are going to be bunking with me and Owen tonight." Jack said, watching the headmistress make her descent. He distrusted that woman. She had to know more than she was letting on.

Emera pulled away and started toward the ladies' hallway, Jack following. Looking in the room, hesaw that all of Ameth's stuff was already gone. He stood outside the door as Emera packed up her stuff. Leaving the lady's hallway and entering the men's, they could hear Ameth talking to Owen. They opened the door, and Ameth jumped and issued a quick, shrill scream. Owen was also startled by their entrance. Emera came in with her stuff and sat it on the floor. "You had the same idea." Owen said.

"Yeah," Jack closed the door behind him and sat in the desk chair. "Something just isn't right about this."

"Really?" Ameth said. "Owen told me what he saw. What the hell was it?"

"I still haven't heard exactly what it was either." Emera said.

"I don't know what you'd call it." Owen said. "Bigfoot maybe?"

"Bigfoot's supposed to be more ape-like." Jack said. "I don't know about you, but I would describe that thing as canine."

"Yeah," Owen agreed.

"Would you just give us a straight answer?" Ameth demanded, getting frustrated.

"There isn't much of a straight answer to give." Jack took in a deep breath and slowly let it out. "In the mid-90's, there was a canine humanoid spotted in Wisconsin. It was called a lot of things, the Wisconsin Werewolf, the Beast of Bray Road, the dogman. Anyway, this thing was spotted for several months in one area and then later in other states. Always at night and near woods."

"Jack, what are you suggesting?" Emera asked, placing her hands on his shoulders and rubbing them slightly.

"Well, we're only a few states removed from Wisconsin. There's plenty of wilderness. What if this is the same thing those people saw? What if it is some unknown species or – God, I can't believe I'm saying this - a werewolf." Jack waited. Emera quit rubbing his shoulders. Ameth sat stupefied. Owen looked at the floor.

"You can't be serious." Ameth said.

"I shot the thing in the shoulder, and it dug the bullet out. You can go look at it on the third floor. I'm very serious." Jack ran his hands through his hair. "After we're done with the police in the morning, I want to pack up and get out of here."

"You can't believe this garbage?" Ameth said, turning to her husband.

"I wish I didn't, but I can't come up with anything that makes more sense." Owen looked at all of them. "Regardless of what it is, I'm with Jack; let's leave and not look back."

As the hours of the night passed, Jack and Owen slept fitfully on the floor, while Emera and Ameth dreamed peacefully on the beds.

Jack awoke from a fevered dream and saw the streaks of daylight crossing the dingy, white ceiling. He smiled at the thought that they were almost out of this place and he looked over and to see Owen staring up at the ceiling also. He was sure that Owen felt the same relief that he did. They lay on the floor, watching the daylight grow brighter as it filled more and more of the room. Shortly before it completely invaded the room, Emera woke up. "Good morning," she said, sitting up in the bed. Raising her hands up over her head and stretching back, she popped her shoulders and back. The noise woke Ameth, who sat up and looked around, taking in her surroundings. From the door came a small timid knock.

"Who is it?" Owen asked.

"It's Ruby." Said a small voice from behind the door.

Jack got up and opened the door for the youngest sister. She was smiling at them, already dressed with her hair brushed. "I thought I should tell you that breakfast will be ready soon."

41

"Thanks Rube," said Emera using her sister's nickname. "Are you ready to go home?"

Ruby just nodded her head. "Can't wait." Ruby looked at her four escorts home and said, "I'll see you guys downstairs."

She turned and skipped down the hall. Her hard soled shoes sent small echoes down the enclosed hallway. Jack grabbed his clothes from his duffel bag, unloaded his pistol and put it back in its case. "We'll give you ladies some privacy and go change at the end of the hall."

Owen scrounged up some clothes and followed Jack down the hall. The hardwood floor was cold on their feet, and the bathroom's pale, lime green tile was no better; two stalls and a urinal were their dressing rooms with an old porcelain sink set into the wall. Jack and Owen sighed and began changing into their clothes for traveling back. They both wore solid-colored t-shirts, but Owen put on a fresh pair of olive green corduroy pants; according to Ameth it went well with the navy blue shirt. Jack put on the same pair of jeans he'd worn the night before and a dark crimson shirt. Owen slid on some tennis shoes, while Jack put on his hiking boots. By the time they got back to the room, the girls had dressed and were almost completely packed. "Shall we go?" Owen asked smiling.

The sunlight was having a profound effect on Owen and Jack. The nightmare they had seen the night before seemed less real, less threatening in the bright warmth of the sunlight. It remained that way as they began their descent down the stairs, until they came to the third floor landing and saw the dried blood and the bullet sitting in the center of it, a stark reminder of last night's terror. The quartet finished their descent and went into the dining room again. The previous night's meal of roast had been replaced with warming trays filled with eggs and hash browns. There were large servers of bacon, and at the end of each table was a tray of assorted breads, muffins, and bagels. There were two glasses placed before each plate setting, one filled with milk, and the other with orange juice. Sitting down, Emera took a sip of her juice and noticed that it was fresh-squeezed. At the head of their table was Ms. Toews, dressed in a different dark dress that came all the way to her throat where it was closed by a single pearl button. She nodded at the guests, who smiled and nodded back. Jack was about to ask for some bacon, when Ms. Toews beckoned him with a finger.

"I've done as you asked young man. The constable will be here within the hour." She said to him. He nodded his understanding and went back to enjoy his breakfast.

As they were finishing their bountiful breakfast, there was a loud, echoing knock from the door. Samantha moved very gracefully to answer it, almost as if she had forgotten the events of the previous night. Jack also had not seen any bandaging on her arm this morning, but he quickly dismissed it. A few moments passed, and Samantha returned, her navy blue skirt swishing back and forth with the motion of her hips as she walked. She leaned over and whispered in Ms. Toew's ear. Nodding, Ms. Toews excused herself from the table. "If you gentlemen would not mind, the constable is here and would like a word with you."

Owen dabbed at the corner of his mouth with the cloth napkin and then set it down in his plate. Jack took one last drink from his juice glass and stood up. Both men followed Ms. Toews to the study. She opened the door and held it open for them to enter. Once inside, she allowed the door to swing closed. Sitting in one of the leather chairs was a man in his mid-fifties; he wore a light blue shirt, which was stretched tight across his large pot belly. He had a receding hair line and a graying mustache, but in his youth, his hair had obviously been a healthy shade of brown. He stood up to greet the men. "Good morning, I'm Constable Perkins." He said,

43

Friedkin's Curse

extending his hand. Each man took it accordingly and introduced themselves. "I understand there was some trouble around here last night."

Owen and Jack took turns explaining what had happened while Constable Perkins wrote everything down on his notepad. Finally, after several minutes and a few pages of notes, the law officer read back through several of his notes and asked, "Do you have a permit for the firearm, Mr. Huston?"

"I do; it's in the case with the pistol." Jack responded. The constable nodded, made a quick notation, and closed his notepad.

He stood up and shook the men's hands again. "Well, thank you for your time." He said and turned to leave.

"Are you going to do anything?" Owen asked. "Don't you want to see the bullet or the chapel?"

"No, I've seen what an eaten carcass looks like. What I am going to do is file this report in my office and make sure that animal control is aware of it." He responded, giving a good-natured smile.

"That's it?" Jack asked. "This thing came in through the roof access door, and would have attacked us, and that's all you're going to do?" The constable's smile disappeared, and red began creeping up the side of his neck and into his cheeks.

"Well frankly, I've been a constable in these parts for thirty years and I've never seen any giant wolf. Furthermore, we've never had any reports of a giant wolf. I'll file your report and pass it along to animal control, because on the off chance that your imaginations didn't run away with you last night and you did actually see something new in the area, we'll be able to track its movements." The constable turned to the door once again. He opened, left, and slammed it behind him.

"What do you think?" Jack asked.

"He thinks we're crazy." Owen said.

Jack just nodded in agreement. "Let's get the girls packed, and get out of here." Jack said, heading for the door.

Jack had been around police officers for most of his life. He knew Perkins type, a small-town lawman, who did not want anyone telling him how to do his job.

Part 2: In the Army Now

The overweight constable adjusted the array of items on his belt as he worked his substantial girth behind the wheel of the standard issue Jeep Cherokee w. Perkins could not believe the audacity of those fellows from the city. Coming into his area, causing a stir, and then telling him how to do his job. "Jackasses." Perkins muttered under his breath. He despised outsiders, especially the know-it-all type.

He put the Jeep in gear and backed it up. Switching it into drive, he drove away, leaving the mammoth estate behind him. He pulled onto the road from the driveway and entered the green canopy of the forest. The light shined through the leaves, giving it a green tint. The woods always seemed dark, especially during the summer when the trees would bloom and block out most of the light. Constable Perkins always hated coming out here. He picked up the handset to his radio and made his initial report to Sophie, a local teenager, who had asked for a job for the summer: part-time dispatcher and secretary. "Roger, Mr. Perkins." Came her response over the faint crackle of the radio receiver. "We had a call come in not too long ago. Seems Judge Thompson is having some trouble; do you want to check it out or should I send one of the boys?"

Perkins held the handset for a moment in thought. Thompson's place was halfway down the road toward Mead's Hall and he was already out that way. He depressed the button to respond to her. "Don't bother anyone else. I'll take care of it. Perkins out."

He put the handset back in its cradle and came upon a turn in the road. The Jeep gripped the road and made the turn masterfully, but Perkins could not believe his eyes. Coming around the next turn were two military

Humvees, with the .50 caliber machine guns mounted on top. After the Humvees were fully around the turn and headed toward him, he saw two larger trucks coming up behind the Humvees. As he passed them, Perkins saw in his rear-view mirror that the back of the trucks were filled with soldiers and that the soldiers were armed. The military convoy seemed to be heading to the school. It was the only place to go this far out on the road. Perkins considered turning around and finding out what was going on, but with all the manpower he had just seen go by, he was willing to bet it would be safer back in town at his office. Without thinking about it, Perkins sped up the Jeep heading for the next turn. As he came around the bend, something darted into the highway in front of him.

He did not get a good look at it, but it stood on two feet, and his first thought was that it was a hunter crossing the road. Swerving to miss it, Perkins hit the shoulder, and the front wheel found the ditch. The passenger side of the Jeep dropped off of the ground and caused it to roll over and land back on its wheels again. Perkins, having never let off the gas, felt all four tires catch and shoot forward into a giant oak, his size causing his seat belt to snap loose as the car came to a jarring stop. He hit the steering wheel, and it broke under his impact as did his sternum. Crossing his arms over his shattered breastbone, he wheezed. He felt the blood when he coughed, and his world became nothing but a mural of pain emanating from his chest. With his right hand, he tried to get the radio to call for help, but he could not find it. Opening his eyes for the first time since the crash, he saw the radio lying in the floorboard almost under the passenger seat. His head throbbed, but he could hear a sound.

It was a painful sound that made his skin crawl. He tried to turn his head to see what was making the noise, but the pain convinced him that the less he moved, the better off he'd be. His driver-side rear view mirror was still attached, he looked into the cracked glass and was frightened by what he saw. A humanoid hand with four fingers and a thumb were scraping down the side of his Jeep. At the end of each finger, was a wicked black claw that scraped off in tiny trails as they drew ever closer to Perkins' door. Covering the hand, wrist, and what little of the forearm that he could see was a dark gray almost black fur. It was rather long, then the claws vanished from his mirror's field of view, and the sound stopped. His window began to fog up. He took a deep breath and turned his head slightly to see what waited outside the door. He started crying despite the pain in his chest, and his bladder and bowels loosened themselves. The door, warped from the wreck, was pulled open and then torn from the car. And the pain in his chest was forgotten as a far worse pain took over as the beast ripped into him with those black claws and feasted on his flesh. Satiated, the monster left behind a scene similar to the one that would have greeted Constable Perkins had he made it to Judge Thompson's house.

General Bridge was in the first Humvee that had passed the constable. Bridge paid little attention to the passing deputy. Local law enforcement was not his concern, nor were they a threat. The past four years had been spent tracking his quarry, never in time to catch it, merely clean up the mess. He had lost many good men over his thirty-year career, but this mission had proved to be a costly one. All of his men had been trained in special combat and weapons, and they all knew what they were up against. This was not their first time to face this foe, but if the intelligence reports were correct, then it was still in the area and had not left a mess to be cleaned up. His driver, Private First Class Royston, kept his steely eyes on the road and his hands on the steering wheel of the Humvee. In the back seat was Specialist Jones. If they ran into trouble, he

Friedkin's Curse

would go up through his hatch and unleash a hell storm of .50 caliber shells on any aggressors.

The men in his squadron were equipped with a standard M-9 sidearm, and most of them had the M-4 carbine while at least a third of them were armed with Mossberg 500 ATP shotguns. Looking at the dossier in his lap one last time, he saw all the information he needed. His base camp was going to be an all-girls academy where the beast had been sighted by several of the students over the previous weeks, and last night, it had actually entered the school. From the report, there had been no casualties, which puzzled Bridge. Of all the attacks they had witnessed, there had not been one without any casualties yet. If his prey was here, it was for one reason; the hunt.

Jack and Owen came down the stairs with the last of Ruby's things in their arms. The trunk of their SUV was packed, but at least they had not needed to devote any seat space to luggage. Ruby was saying good bye to her friends. Emera and Ameth stood by the door waiting. Emera reached her hand into her pocket and felt something cold and metallic. With a puzzled look on her face, she removed the silver chain with the wolf's head pendant on it. "Guys, I've got to give this to Samantha." Hurrying down one of the hallways, Emera kept her eyes out for Samantha.

There were a few students in the halls, but most of them had decided that after the excitement of last night, they wanted to stay in their rooms. Simone was in the kitchen, laying out plates for lunch. "Excuse me, have you seen Samantha?" Emera asked.

Simone stopped what she was doing and thought about it for a minute. Emera could not be sure, but Simone seemed to be distracted. "I saw her in the study." Simone finally said.

"Thanks," Emera said, excusing herself and heading toward the study.

The large wooden door opened seamlessly. Looking in, Emera saw Samantha sitting at a small table. In front of her was a large book, but Samantha did not seem to actually be reading it. Making her way to the teacher, Emera noticed that Samantha had that same loss of focus as Simone. *Most likely because of last night,* Emera thought to herself.

The rubber sole of Emera's sneaker made a slight squeaking noise, and Samantha looked up as if she had been caught in the middle of a daydream. She shook off the slightly confused look and smiled. "Weren't you leaving?"

"In just a minute." Emera said. "We found this last night in the cellar and thought it might be yours." Emera held out her hand, revealing the chain and pendant.

Samantha gasped and slapped Emera's hand, causing the chain and pendant to sail across the room. "Get that away from me!" She said, in a breathy deep voice. Emera took a step back as she saw the wild look cross Samantha's face. As quickly as it had come, it left. "I'm sorry. After last night, that horrible face scared me."

Her voice had returned to normal, but Emera wanted to leave the room just in case Samantha freaked out again. "It's okay. So, it's not yours?" Emera asked, backing over to where the chain had landed. She kneeled and picked it up.

"No, it's not. Again, I'm sorry." Samantha said, but Emera couldn't help but feel that this was a facade. The real Samantha was the one who had slapped her hand.

"It's no problem. I'll let you get back to your reading." Emera said as she put the chain back in her pocket and backed towards the open door.

51

Once she had left the library, she closed the door behind her. It took all her restraint to not run as fast as she could back to the others.

They were by the door where they had been a minute ago. The only difference was that Ruby had joined them, and the men no longer held any of her stuff. Emera assumed they had finished loading the car. Jack's smile faded when he saw Emera's face. "What happened?"

Emera forced a smile. "Nothing. It's not hers. So, we ready?"

"Yes," Ameth said.

Ms. Toews stood at the foot of the steps, presumably to see them off. Jack let the others go out first. Owen stopped on the front steps and looked up, listening. The others heard it as well. It was the sound of heavy diesel engines.

Royston finally broke the silence inside the Humvee. "Sir, destination is just ahead."

Bridge looked up and closed the file. He could see the end of the forest line and a brick structure beyond it. When they pulled out of the forest, Bridge realized this was not the end of the tree line but merely a small clear patch in the middle of the forest. The school was bigger than his initial reports had indicated. Standing on the front steps were a little girl - most likely one of the students - and four adults, the oldest not even thirty. He sized them up and did not sense any particular threat from them. The Humvee stopped by the steps, and Bridge put on his best public smile. He opened the door to the Humvee and stepped out into the late morning air. "Good morning. I'm General Bridge." He held his hand out to the men first, then the women, and finally the girl. "I hope you weren't planning on leaving just yet."

"We were going to go home." Owen offered. His throat went dry as the men started piling out of the trucks with their weapons.

Jack noticed that they seemed to be breaking into groups of four and forming a small perimeter around the front of the building. "I'm afraid the United States government needs your cooperation." Bridges said, still wearing the smile that never made it to his eyes. "We have a situation and are not going to be able to permit anyone to leave for the next twenty-four to forty-eight hours."

Jack stared back at Bridge, who was getting a sense that this man might be trouble. "What type of situation?" Jack asked.

"I'm afraid I'm not at liberty to discuss that, but I assure you we just need you to stay here while we deal with the situation." Bridge continued smiling. And with every second, Jack and Owen distrusted the man with two stars on his collar less and less. "Now, if you wouldn't mind going back inside."

Jack took a step toward the car and noticed the nearest group of soldiers raising their rifles. Bridge put his hand on Jack's chest and halted him. "Son, that's not the way inside."

Jack did not flinch or back down. "No, it's the way to our clothes and toiletries. Since you are holding us here, we would at least like a change of clothes and our toothbrushes."

Bridge's smile widened even more. "Of course," he said, slapping Jack on the back. The soldiers relaxed and placed their rifles back at their sides. "I like you, kid; you got guts." This was a lie; Bridge had a sudden contempt for this man.

Jack knew he was pushing his luck going for the car, but if these guys were here, Jack was willing to bet it had something to do with what happened last night. His pistol was in his duffel bag, and he wanted that nearby if he was going to be stuck here. Owen followed him to the car.

"What is the meaning of this?" Ms. Toews asked, stepping around the group of visitors.

"Hello, ma'am, you must be the administrator of this fine school." Bridge said stepping past Ameth and Emera. "I'm General Bridge, United States Army. We need your full cooperation as we try to contain a hazardous situation."

"Certainly," Ms. Toews said, never looking away from the soulless emerald eyes of Bridge. "Though I still do not understand why you have come here, unannounced."

"Well, ma'am, I'm on a very classified mission. I'd tell you about it, but it's a matter of national security; my men and I are going to need a base camp and will need the use of your dormitories."

"If I refuse?" She asked defiantly.

"I would hope that you would not do that. Having my men here will ensure that you don't have any more situations like the one you had last night." Bridge's smile vanished. "I'm sure the safety of your students and staff is your utmost concern."

"It most certainly is." Ms. Toews said matter of factly.

"Let me put your mind to ease; we will keep contact with them at a minimum and we will do our best not to disrupt the daily routines of anyone here." Bridge stared at Ms. Toews, boring into her with his eyes. Emera stood silently watching; it seemed as if Ms. Toews was shrinking, her shoulders sagging. The fight had gone out of her.

"Very well," she said. "Your men can occupy the fourth floor where our guest rooms are located."

Bridge nodded at her. "We'll also need a larger room for communications." He said.

"There is a chapel on that floor that should serve your purpose." Ms. Toews turned and walked inside the school. As the door began shutting, Emera heard Ms. Toews say: "Get the students into the auditorium; I have an announcement to make."

Jack and Owen were back with the luggage that they had already loaded in the car once. Emera and Ameth walked back up the steps, opened the door, and led the way as the men followed with the bags. Bridge stood on the stone steps looking into the forest. He put a cigar to his lips and lit the tip, inhaling the acrid, burning smoke and letting it fill his lungs before exhaling out his nose. "All right, boys," he called. "Bunks on the fourth floor. I want a reconnaissance of the building: weak points, fortification areas and so on. Communications will be on four with us. Find someone to show you the chapel, Wierzbowski. I want radio and satellite uplink five minutes ago." Wierzbowski, the communication's officer, nodded his head and began loading gear onto a cart. The general continued barking orders. "Lieutenant Canva, take a squad; I want full motion detectors on the perimeter and infrared at all access points." Canva, the tallest man in the squad pointed out three men around him and gave a thumb toward the back of one of the trucks. The lieutenant stood out from the other men, not just because of his size but he was also Hawaiian.

The men pulled out rolled pieces of canvas lined inside with small rope clasps that held a long, metal shaft pointed at one end with a small, yellow attachment with a clear face plate at the other end. It was a motion sensor unit. Once the perimeter was lined, there would be no way in or out without the men knowing it. Canva scooped half of the contents of the

Friedkin's Curse

first canvas into his arms and began walking, placing them ever three steps. He had learned after his first mission with the squad that the motion detectors had to be overlapping. On that first mission, they had not, and it had gotten to them. Canva still carried the scar on his shoulder, where he had been clawed. While he was lying in shock from his wound, he watched as his superior, the man he had replaced afterwards, was torn limb from limb, screaming in a high pitched wail for mercy. Canva would not make the same mistake as that man. Looking over his shoulder, Canva made sure the men were placing the detectors correctly. The men had seen him do the drill enough times that they should be used to it now. Examining the progression of the perimeter, he went back to his work. Bridge saw the perimeter going up and watched as the men not assigned any other task piled in to find a bunk, rifles shouldered and duffel bags at their side.

Ameth, Emera, Owen and Jack had just gotten back into their room, having left Ruby with the other students in the auditorium when they heard the ordered march of hard-soled military boots coming up the stairs. Jack closed the door, slid a chair against it, and sat down. "I think these guys are here because of what we saw last night." Owen said, breaking the silence.

"It's too big of a coincidence for it to be anything else." Jack said. "The question is why? Bridge seems too anxious to get at this; I think he's faced it before."

"How?" Ameth asked.

"Think about it; he's throwing around national security to keep from answering any real questions. He shows up the day after the school is broken into. Owen, what are they doing?"

Owen looked out the window as the sound of boots went down the hall on the women's side and then turned away. "They're putting some kind of posts up. It looks like they have some kind of sensor on them."

"Lights?" Emera suggested.

"I don't think so," Owen said.

"They also happen to be heavily armed." Jack said, concluding his argument. "They would not send this many men for a small threat, and really what threat can be out here? It's not exactly like the hills are teeming with people."

"I know," Ameth said. "It just seems so far-fetched that. . ."

Someone pushed on the door, cutting Ameth's sentence short. "Open up," came a male voice, impatient and gruff.

There was a harder push on the door, and this time Jack and the chair moved a little bit. Jack stood up and slid the chair out of the way. The door opened, and there stood two soldiers. One of them was just as tall as Jack and thick while the other one was shorter and much slimmer. The tall soldier looked in and smiled.

"I like this room; do they come with it?" The tall soldier said, giving a leer at the women. Owen read the name tag above the shirt pocket, Jonas, it said.

Jack stepped in front of Jonas. "This room's taken, and they don't go anywhere." Jack said. Owen moved up a few steps to stand just off of Jack's right.

The soldier dropped his duffel bag, and slid his M-4 assault rifle off his shoulder and handed it to his smaller companion. Jonas stood toe-to-toe with Jack, their noses almost touching. "What are you going to do if I say different?" Jonas asked, smiling.

Jack smiled back, took a half step back with his left foot, and slammed his forehead into Jonas' nose. There was a sickening crunch, and the man fell backwards out of the doorway, blood flowing from his freshly broken nose. On Jack's forehead was a splatter of blood from the impact; the little man just stared with his mouth gaping open while Jonas reached for his sidearm. Jack knew there was no way he could stop him before he could draw and pull the trigger, but he didn't have to. A black combat boot kicked the man in the side of the head. Jonas rolled over onto his stomach and covered his head. It was Bridge. "What's the meaning of this?" He demanded.

Jonas and his friend remained silent, but Owen spoke up. "These men sought to evict us from this room and . . . implied some less than respectful ideas as to how they could entertain themselves." Owen indicated Emera and Ameth with his hand.

Bridge looked at the four civilians in the room and the two soldiers, one of which had tried to draw a weapon on an unarmed man. "Get up," Bridge ordered, and Jonas stood up. "You two are not to get anywhere near ANY civilian on these premises. If you do, I'll see to it that you are personally taken into the woods and shot. Do I make myself clear?"

"Sir, yes sir!" Answered the two soldiers.

"Now, go find bunks at the far end of that other hall. If someone else is in them, tell them I said those were your bunks now." The men ran down the hall to get out from under the angry gaze of Bridge. He took off his hat and stepped into the door. "I'm terribly sorry. If you have any other problems, find me or one of my sergeants."

He stepped back out the door, pulling it to behind him. One crisis averted. The Pentagon made it perfectly clear: civilian casualties are acceptable but only in the event that they are converted into a hostile force. Bridge would not let anything jeopardize his mission, even if he thought Jack did deserve to be taught a lesson. He watched as the soldiers made quick strides down the hall. Jonas and the little man, Wickes, had been implicated in several instances of improper conduct with female civilians. Bridge would have to keep a closer eye on them. From the small earphone in his ear, came a small burst of static followed by one word: "General?"

He pulled a cord up to put the microphone near his mouth. "This is Bridge, over."

"Sir, the perimeter is complete. We have uplink and satellite feeds of the surrounding area." Wierzbowski said.

"Good, how long do we have satellite?" Bridge asked. The satellite had come in handy in the past for detecting larger than anticipated nests of hostile creatures.

Wierzbowski, his pale shaved head reflecting the light of the monitor, made a few clicks on his keyboard and then spoke into his own microphone. "It appears we'll have satellite until 0200 hours. We'll then have a six-hour blackout."

Bridge did not like this; it would be the heart of the night, which time had proven if nothing else was feeding time for these things. Pondering over the situation and forming a defense strategy, Bridge continued walking down the hall, inspecting the men and their chosen bunks. Jack, Owen, Emera, and Ameth left their room, closing the door behind them. They saw the general continuing down the hallway and started in the opposite direction, towards the stairs.

They passed several soldiers on each landing. It appeared that they were setting a guard on each floor. As they came to the foyer, several soldiers were placing sandbags outside on the steps building a small

59

fortification, and in the center a tripod mounted M-249 light machine gun, which could easily be picked up and redistributed if needs be. Owen was wondering why they had such a piece of equipment, with the Humvees having the larger .50 cal machine guns. Jack looked at it and assumed it was for use in the event that the Humvees were preoccupied with other targets or if it was needed somewhere inaccessible to the Humvees. The large trucks had been parked across the front of the house, blocking most of the front windows and boxing in the front steps.

Emera led the way from the main room to Ms. Toews office, stopped in front of an ornate cherry -colored door, and gave a light knock. "Come in." Came the response from the other side.

Turning the golden doorknob, they found Ms. Toews seated in a high-backed dark cherry colored leather chair behind an imposing wooden desk. The desk was neat, nothing out of place. Among other things, a small round cup that matched the color of the desk and contained several pencils and pens sat to one side, a few papers were stacked neatly to the side, and a black phone sat on the far left corner of the desk. Beyond that, there was nothing on her desk; the walls held a few modest pieces of art that were not memorable, both landscapes. Placed directly behind her desk was a large window, almost as wide as the desk itself. The thick, iron bars were used to actually hold the glass in place. It was obvious that the window was especially made for this room. On both sides of the window were framed documents that at a glance looked to be college degrees and certifications. There was a large bookcase with glass doors on the wall directly across from her desk that appeared to be filled with antique books. Sitting in front of the bookcase were two more chairs to match hers. She smiled at them as they filed in one by one. The smell of the leather mixed with the real wood furniture and gave the room a classic smell.

Emera and Ameth sat down in the chairs while the men stood behind them. "I take it this is about our latest arrivals." She said.

Emera nodded. "Where's Ruby?"

"I had her and the rest of the children escorted back to their rooms. All those soldiers, I did not want one of the children getting underfoot." The headmistress explained.

"Do you have any idea what's going on?" Jack asked. She just shook her head. "Do you have any idea why that thing is hanging around here? Anything that might shed some light on this?"

She hesitated for a moment. "Young man, I may, but I assure you that I think it is foolishness." She reached into her top desk drawer and pulled out an old, leather-bound book. The pages were yellowed and curled with age. "This is the journal of General Friedkin, the man who built this grand house." She pulled another antique book out, but this one was newer than the journal. "This belonged to a tobacco farmer who tried to settle here in the early part of the 20th century."

Jack picked up the books and placed them under his arm. "What am I going to find?"

"Rantings of great men who suffered under the duress of their own legends." She replied.

Simone opened the door and stepped in. "Ms. Toews. . ." she started, stopping herself once she saw the others.

Simone's face was troubled, tears apparently threatening to spill from her eyes. "What's wrong?" Ms. Toews asked.

"Some of the soldiers." Simone paused. "They're beastly. Samantha and I have heard some of the crudest things from them."

"Yeah, we had a run-in with a couple of them before we came down here." Owen said, listening as the ceiling creaked from the soldiers walking above them. "I'd be careful; they seem to be a rough group."

"Rough or not, they are guests in my school." Ms. Toews said, standing up behind the desk. "Simone, go find General Bridge and tell him that I demand to see him at once."

Simone nodded and left the room. "You may want to call the constable back out here." Ameth added.

Ms. Toews reached for the phone and picked up the handset. With a baffled look, she hung up the phone. "It seems the line is down."

Jack looked out the window at the soldiers passing by with large bolt and wire cutters in hand. "Down nothing, they were cut. They don't want us getting word out that they're here."

"Nonsense." Ms. Toews said. "It happens all the time out here. I'll simply have General Bridge get one of his men to take me into town. From there, I'll get our attorney and the constable both out here to make sure that everything is done legitimately."

The four guests filed out of the room and went back upstairs. Owen led the way up the stairs with Ameth and Emera behind him and Jack bringing up the rear. The soldiers did not give them a second notice as they passed the checkpoints on the landings, and once on the hall, none of the soldiers seemed to take much notice of them. Owen and Jack both noticed a few quick glances at them, but nothing significant. Apparently, word of Jack's encounter with Jonas had spread. They entered their room and closed the door behind them. Owen and Jack pulled one of the beds to where it would block the door, just in case anyone tried to intrude. Jack pulled the table that had served as a nightstand and sat it against the wall opposite the door, using it for a chair this time.

General Bridge came in from his inspection of the vehicles to see Ms. Toews, not knowing what to expect from the woman. She had seemed easy enough to intimidate into letting them use her school as a base of operations. He arrived at the door, which had been indicated to him as her office and found her sitting behind her desk, awaiting his arrival. She motioned with her hand for him to take a seat across from him. He sat down and removed his hat. "What can I do for you, ma'am?" He asked, remembering sitting on this side of a principal's desk when he was a teenager. The thought made his palms a little sweaty.

"Your men need to mind their manners, if I am to cooperate with your endeavor." She simply stated. "I have been informed that they have made lewd comments toward my associates, students, and our guests."

Bridge clenched his fist beside his chair, his anger burning inside him. Her impetuous question of his methods and his command made his blood boil. The salesman smile he had cultivated over his long career still remained on his face as he nodded to the old woman's words. "I'll be sure to have a talk with the men and let them know that inappropriate behavior will not be tolerated. Please be sure to notify me if there is anything else."

Bridge began to stand, until Ms. Toews cleared her throat. The general looked at her and realized that the conversation was not over. He lowered himself back into the chair. "We also seem to be having some trouble with our phone lines."

Standard Operating Procedure was to silence all ground communications, so Bridge had ordered his men to sever the lines providing any phone or internet access as well as to use their cellular signal jammers. The last thing he or the government wanted was publicity; some things were best left unknown. General Bridge had been told early on to keep the mission in the black, which meant one simple thing: don't let people outside the contact zone know. "That is a shame, but I don't see what I could possibly do to help." The general said, but before he could even begin to stand, Ms. Toews began.

"I'd like you to have one of your men drive me into town." Ms. Toews stared into the general and saw no noticeable reaction. "Given the circumstances of your arrival, I would like to have our legal representative here."

"Legal representative?" Bridge asked.

"This institution has a fine lawyer in Mead Hall. I would appreciate if I could get your men to drive into town to contact him and I could ride back with him. I may also see if I can have a constable accompany me back." She said matter-of-factly. "Is that going to be a problem?"

"None," Bridge squinted his eyes at something on the back wall. "What is that?" He asked, pointing.

Ms. Toews turned around and saw where he was indicating. Walking to where she believed he was pointing, she inquired. "This?" He nodded, coming to stand beside her. "Well, that's my certificate for lifetime achievement in education." She laughed a little bit to herself. "Funny story."

Then, a firm, callused hand wrapped over her throat, preventing any sound from escaping, and she felt a sharp pin prick just to the right of her lower back. She struggled, trying to breathe, and clawed at the hand holding her throat. The steel grip did not budge. Her vision started to blacken around the edges, she felt light headed, and suddenly, an extreme chill set up in her body. Her vision continued to darken until it appeared as if she was falling down a well. Her body went limp against the general.

He maintained the grip on her throat for another full minute and then laid her down on her stomach and removed the combat knife from her back. He had stabbed directly into her renal arteries and then moved the tip of the blade at an angle side to side to do as much damage as possible, speeding the woman along to her final rest. He spoke into the microphone hanging inside his shirt. "Private Royston, Specialist Jones, report to me in the headmistress' office on the double and bring a bag." He let the microphone drop.

Within seconds, he could hear the men hurrying down the hall. They opened the door and stood at attention. "At ease," said the general. "Now get in here and close that door. Did you bring the bag?"

Jones pulled the thick black bag out from under his vest. "Yes sir."

"Good. Bring it over here; you boys are going on a dump run." The men came around the desk and saw the old woman with the knife wound in her back. The men laid out the bag and transferred her from the floor to the unzipped body bag. Bridge cleaned the gore off of his knife on the back of Ms. Toews' dress. "Now we can't have anyone outside the unit see this. Royston, you go make sure it's clear, and Jones, you'll carry her out. Once she's secured in the back of the Humvee drive halfway back to town and dump her. Wait until enough time has passed and then come back; we need these people thinking that she's staying in town. Understood?"

Both replied in unison: "Sir, yes, sir."

Jones zipped up the bag, hiding the body. Royston took a few tentative steps out of the room and motioned for Jones to follow. They were fortunate; the students were in their rooms, and the remaining faculty was elsewhere. Royston still kept a watchful eye out for any unwanted

Friedkin's Curse

attention. They made it to the Humvee without incident and without being seen by anyone but their fellow soldiers. Jones sat in the back, while Royston drove away at a normal, calm pace.

Jack and the others heard the Humvee fire up its engine. Looking out the small window, they saw the Humvee exit the school. "Maybe now we'll find out what's going on." Jack said.

"I hope so." Emera responded.

Ameth sat on the bed, pressing on the smooth touch screen of her iPhone. "Me too." She sighed and put the phone back into her pocket. "I can't pick up anything."

"Yeah, you lose signal shortly after you leave Mead's Hall." Owen said, rubbing his eyes. "I noticed it the first time that I came up here to take care of the network."

Jack hopped off of the table and emptied his bag on the floor; he found the case for his revolver and opened it. He wanted to make sure that there were no bullets left inside to accidentally fire. He then removed a long, slender brush with an iron wool pyramid at the top. With care, he began pushing the pyramid into the barrel and bullet slots in the cylinder, repeating the procedure several times. Finally, he held it up and examined the places he had brushed. He then took six shells and loaded the pistol, firmly pushing the cylinder in place until he heard the click assure him it was in place. He sat the pistol on the floor beside him and laid his head back against the leg of the table. He noticed that everyone was watching him. "Sorry." He said. "I'm tired and didn't want to wait until tonight to deal with that. I'm going to try and get some sleep."

Jack raised himself off of the floor, holding the revolver, and made his way over to the bed that remained in its original position. Emera stood up. "Lay down, babe." She told him. He lied down on his side with his back to the wall. "What do we do if some of the soldiers try to get in?"

"They won't, and if they do, the bed is against the door. We'll have plenty of warning." Jack slowly closed his eyes, the pistol tucked into the back of his pants, held in place by his belt. "Something may happen tonight, so you guys may want to get some shut-eye, too."

Owen nodded. "Yeah, I'm beat." He lied down on his back, and Ameth nuzzled into his side.

Emera lied down in front of Jack and he curled an arm around her, pulling her against him. It was comforting, but Emera admitted to herself that this was scary and something bad might happen. Jack's breath was light on her hair and calmed her as it softly caressed the back of her neck. She smiled and forgot her worries, if only for the moment. And the friends slept soundly with the soldiers outside the door going about their business, readying weapons and building defenses.

Jonas and Wickes were in their room, Wickes with his hands behind his head staring at the ceiling and daydreaming about women. Jonas, however, was not so relaxed. He was stalking the room, furious. His nose had stopped bleeding but then started swelling. He was having trouble breathing through it, and his head was killing him from where Bridge had kicked him. "I swear, man," he said to Wickes. "I get a chance, that asshole is dead. I'll bag him and just chalk it up to friendly fire."

"Jonas," Wickes responded. "Don't worry about him, man; think about those two teachers and our lady friends down the hall." Wickes licked his lips and let his vile imagination run wild with the possibilities.

"To hell with that." Jonas said, raising Wickes from his perverse daydreams. "He broke my nose, and to top it off, the General's going to be on our ass."

"Calm down, man." Wickes urged. It scared him when Jonas got angry because Jonas was a violent, unstable man, and Wickes knew it. "We'll get our chance to get even, just wait."

"Even?" Jonas said the word as if he were chewing it around his mouth, and then made a face that indicated that he found it bitter. "I don't want even; I want him dead. One shot is all I need." Jonas' voice raose to a fever pitch, his bloodlust building with every passing second.

There was a knock at the door, and Jonas opened it to a broad-shouldered black man with three stripes on his uniform, indicating his rank as a sergeant. His face was blank and emotionless, which made is all the more surprising when, Jonas went sprawling on the floor from Sergeant Wiine shoving him in the chest with one hand. The movement was so quick that Wickes almost didn't register it as a movement. One minute, Jonas was there, and the next, he was moving and an open hand had taken his place. "I don't care, Jonas. The guy down the hall? You let your personal shit go. You want to even things up, you do it when you aren't in uniform, and since you didn't bring any other outfit, you'll be doing it somewhere else. We have orders." Wiine stared down at the man, those dark lifeless eyes boring holes directly through Jonas. "Understand?"

"Yes, Sergeant," Jonas managed in between his gasps for air.

"Also, the walls aren't as thick as you think, so keep your thoughts to yourself." Wiine pulled the door shut and left the two men to their thoughts. Wickes went back to his daydreams, and Jonas lay on the floor, trying to catch his breath all the while calculating how to end the guy who had busted his face.

Lieutenant Canva stood watch behind the sand bag wall in front of the main entrance. The M-249 stood to his right; behind it was a Private he did not know. Taking a quick sideways glance, Canva read the man's name above his shirt pocket: Sands. Sands was on alert, his eyes darting back and forth, waiting for something to move against them so he could unleash the long strands of ammunition that glittered in the sunlight like pieces of gold. This was most likely Sands third mission. Canva had witnessed eight previous attempts at capture, and each one had been a failure, some with more bloodshed than others. Night-time was when you had to be alert, other than the primary target; there was not a known hostile agent who could attack in the daylight. At least they had not encountered any yet, Canva decided to tell the kid, he would need to preserve his energy. "Hey, you can lighten that grip on the trigger, son. Things won't get nasty until the sun sets. We're out here just in case, plus it keeps the men from getting into mischief."

Sands chuckled. "I saw the mischief I wanted to get into." He looked over his shoulder and gave a quick nod.

Canva looked and saw the teacher from earlier, the one with her hair pulled back into a bun, and the other one with her hair pulled into a pony tail. Canva had to admit the kid had taste. "Sands, you know the rules about engaging civvies in any type of non-mission related activity."

Sands blushed a little bit. "Yes, sir." Sands turned his head back to the forest and pressed the M-249 firmly against his shoulder.

The small talk was finished. Canva kept scanning the woods, just in case. They had lost two men one mission when Hostile Zero attacked in broad daylight. It had leaped from the woods and landed on both of them. Only one man had been able to scream, but that was because the other's jaw had been pulled from his face before his body ever hit the ground. Canva shuddered to remember the thought, glistening bone, spurting blood, and the man's wet tongue dangling. The memory shook Canva from his confident attitude, and he thumbed off the safety of his M-4 and scanned the woods in earnest.

General Bridge sat in the leather chair behind Ms. Toews desk. He liked it. He had to admit the woman had taste; shame he had to remove her from the equation. Still, if everything went well, then there would be no problems with her disappearance. In all the times they had been close, their prey had sprung the trap and escaped. This time . . . felt different. Bridge welcomed an end to this hunt; he had found his white whale with this. The mission had been given to him specifically, and he relished it. The danger and cunning of his opponent made Bridge hunt that much harder, hounding every inch of the journey. Always too late to stop the carnage, but never too late to pick the trail up. This was the first place that the damage had not already been done, most likely because of whatever occurred to repel the beast.

Something in his blood told him that this was going to be the time. He had never been as sure as he was at this moment. The beast would be in their hands before week's end. It had come to this specific place, and it seemed to want to stay here. Most likely, it was the forest. It provided shelter and a wide food resource, yet somehow it had still come to the humans. Having tasted human flesh before, Bridge assumed the beast had a taste for it. And there was the other issue with their mission, the act they needed to prevent if they could find the host. However, the target had to identify the host, and so far, they had seen or heard of no indication of that happening.

Bridge flipped through the pages of notes he'd taken during his long hunt. It was changing things up, doing something strange. Bridge did not like it, but he had a strong feeling that would be the undoing of his foe.

Jones and Royston were heading toward town, when they came upon the Constable's Jeep Cherokee. It had smashed headfirst into a tree. Judging from how deep in the engine the tree was, the constable had never hit the brakes. Royston slowed the Humvee and came to a complete halt. "What do you think?" He asked over his shoulder to Jones, raising his voice to get over the growl of the engine.

Jones leaned over the seat; his dark skin merged well with the shadows in the back. "I'll cover you. Check it out. We may be able to just dump her here." Jones leaned back over the seat and climbed into his position behind the .50 caliber. He turned with the weapon in a full circle, making sure that there was not any hostile movement toward them. "GO!" He ordered.

Royston opened the door to the Humvee, quickly got out, and racked the bolt on his M-4. It was prepped and ready. Royston made his way around the front of the Humvee, feeling the heat coming off of the massive engine block as it rose out through the hood and grill of the vehicle. He maintained his M-4 in a firing position with the stock drawn tight to his shoulder in case this was a trap. Jones sat in his perch, maintaining the .50 caliber near Royston's position, but his head kept turning around to maintain a 360 degree lookout. The Cherokee was destroyed and would not be salvageable. The driver's side door lay off to the side; it had probably come off in the impact. Maintaining his cautious approach, Royston noticed the scratch marks down the side of the

Cherokee, its paint peeled back where four lines had been carved into the paint all the way down to where the door should have been.

Neither Royston nor Jones thought the Constable was still alive. Blood was visible on the rear windows and windshield through the cargo door. It also was dripping out of the driver's side of the car, where the door once had been. There was also a large puddle of congealed blood beneath the Cherokee. Taking a tentative step around the massive puddle of blood, Royston looked in and saw the carnage. His mind did not at first register that what he was looking at had been human, except for the few scraps of clothes left and the head. Other than that, it looked like a side of beef. Constable Perkins' immense stomach had been ripped open and devoured. Royston could see parts of his intestines in the floor board, but the man's legs were missing. One of his arms was also gone, and the other one was detached and lay on the dashboard. It was obvious that it had not happened when he hit the tree; from the white glistening ball of bone showing, something had ripped the arm out and Royston assumed the tissue damage was when the arm had been partially eaten. The smell of putrification with the earthy smell of the forest was overpowering.

Royston felt the heat rising into his face, and the acid creeping up his esophagus. He turned and ran from the car to vomit into the deep vegetation. His ears were ringing as he retched several times. Once the stomach convulsions had stopped, Royston heard the booming bass voice of Jones. He stood up and wiped his mouth with the back of his hand. Once he'd cleaned the corners of his mouth, he turned around to face the gunner. "Royston, what's wrong with you?" Jones looked over his shoulders and then looked back to Royston. "We've seen it before."

Royston shook his head. "I've never seen this before." He explained, pointing to the cab of the Cherokee. "But we'll put her here. We'll be out of here before anyone finds her."

Heading back to the Humvee, Royston felt like something was watching him. He slung the rifle over his shoulders so he could easily grip the trigger and fire if he had to. From the way that Jones was scanning the forest, Royston knew that he felt it, too. Something out there was watching them. Possibly as it had watched the constable.

Opening the rear hatch of the Humvee, Royston grabbed the body bag and drug it out onto the hard asphalt of the road. He unzipped the bag and revealed the headmistress, Ms. Toews. Neither Royston nor Jones knew what had happened between her and the General, and neither one cared. They were good soldiers, followed every order without question. Sliding her body out of the body bag, Royston slipped his arms under her shoulders and around her chest. He pulled and dragged her from the highway to the side of the Cherokee, then He half-tossed half-twisted her so that she fell face first in the pile of blood congealing on the vegetation. It was enough; something would most likely take care of her out in the forest. Royston went and collected the body bag, put it inside the rear of the Humvee, and closed the hatch.

Thankful to finally be done with the chore so that he could leave this place where an unseen enemy had watched their every move, Royston pulled the M-4 off of his shoulder and tossed it into the passenger seat. He put the Humvee in reverse, made a quick, short effort of turning the massive vehicle around in the middle of the road, and pressed the accelerator, speeding back to the school. Jones ducked back inside from the turret and closed it off. "Good work, soldier." Jones said, slapping him on the shoulder.

Royston put on a nervous smile. Despite the eighteen months he'd been driving for the General, he still wasn't overly comfortable with the men in the unit, except Jones. "Thanks, man. 'Preciate the cover." He said back to Jones.

"No problem," was Jones' reply.

The rumble of the Humvee's engine woke Emera. She slid away from Jack and stretched, raising her arms above her head and trying not to disturb the others. Going to the window, she saw the Humvee emerge from the canopy of trees. It rumbled to its former place along the front of the school, and the engine cut off. Glancing at her watch, Emera noticed that they had only been gone about forty-five minutes. It had taken them almost that long to reach the school from the outskirts of Mead's Hall. Her first thought was that Ms. Toews had decided against going into town and returned, but the only people that emerged from the vehicle were the soldiers that she had seen inside it earlier. The more stern-looking black soldier reentered the Humvee and climbed into the turret mounted atop of the Humvee to watch the tree line. Her brow furrowed in worry, when she heard a groggy voice behind her. "What's wrong, babe?" It was Jack.

He still lay on the bed and had not moved from the position he had been in when she woke up. "I don't know. Ms. Toews' ride is back."

Jack slowly sat up, still under the heavy blanket of sleep. "How long did we sleep?"

"It's been about thirty minutes since we lied down. They were only gone for forty-five minutes." Emera walked away from the window and sat on the bed, which made a slight groan.

Jack closed his eyes in concentration. "That's not right. They couldn't have gone to town and back in that little of time. Did Ms. Toews come back with them?"

"No, she never got out. I think they did something to her." Emera was truly concerned for the woman. She had not been the most personable individual, but Emera hadn't wished anything bad upon her.

"Whatever it is, we can't do anything about it now. They've got us right where they want us." Jack laid his head back down on the pillow. "I hate to say it, but come back to sleep and we'll sort this out later."

"You can't be serious. Those men hurt her or worse, and you want to go to sleep." Emera was growing furious.

"Em, I don't want anything to happen to her any more than you do. That doesn't change the fact though that we are essentially trapped here. We'll have to choose our time wisely and then find the truth out for ourselves." Jack rubbed the back of her neck as he spoke, and Emera closed her eyes and relaxed to his massaging touch and soothing, baritone voice. "Let's just get some rest and make sure we're ready for whatever happens."

She conceded; Jack did have a valid point. They were all exhausted and needed to rest before they did anything. She lied back down beside Jack and curled up against the warmth of his body.

Royston reported his findings. Jones had remained perched in the .50 caliber nest on the Humvee. General Bridge sat behind the solid desk that had belonged to Ms. Toews, his hands folded in front of his face as he listened. He did not move until Royston finished. Then he raised an eyebrow. "Is that all?" He asked.

Royston saluted. "Yes sir."

General Bridge sat thinking for a moment longer, and then a smile spread across his face. This one was different; it was actually a smile because he was happy. It sent a small chill down Royston's spine. Eighteen months, and he had never seen that smile. It made him severely uncomfortable. "Well, that's good, soldier." The General said, laying his hands down on the arms of the office chair. "Looks like the constable won't be coming out here, then."

"Sir, what about any other constables in town?" Royston felt sweat starting to form under his cap, not from heat but rising anxiety.

"I'll take care of that, son. Report back to your post." Royston saluted, Bridge returned the salute, and the soldier left the office, closing the door behind him. As the door closed with a slightly audible click, Bridge retrieved his earpiece and microphone. Placing them in his ear, he heard several different strands of chatter between the men, mainly reporting no sightings. "This is General Bridge; any unidentified vehicles are to be stopped by any means necessary and any non-hostiles in those vehicles are to be detained here. Squad leaders repeat back."

Bridge listened as his squad leaders repeated back the orders he had just issued. There were no foreseeable complications as of yet. Tonight would be the real test, though. He put a cigar in his mouth and lit the tip until it glowed evenly. He took a breath, feeling the smoke fill his mouth with that slight burn he had come to enjoy so much. He blew out the smoke and smiled. This time, he and his men were ready and the beast would come back. There was no other human establishment nearby.

Jack woke up and saw the dark forest outside the window. His first thought was that it was already night. When he saw the orange glow emanating still, he knew that the sun had merely crossed over the house and was beginning its descent to the horizon. Soon, night would be upon them.

Inside the halls and on the grounds of the school, the soldiers tensed, aware that their target was more active at night. Wickes was just leaving the room at the end of the hall when he noticed the teacher with the glasses and dark hair walking down the hall. Wickes watched her head to the door set into the wall that led onto the stairway to the roof. He watched not suspiciously but merely admiring her frame and the way it moved. The door closed as the sound of her shoes ascending the steps entered into the hallway. Once the door clicked in place, no other sound came through. Not thinking further of it, Wickes headed back down the hall to the main staircase so he could get some chow before starting his guard duty. If memory served, there were a couple of guys on the roof, so the teacher should be fine.

Canva stood at the ready, his M-4 switched from single to burst, and his eyes moved through the ever-deepening darkness for signs of an attack or just a glimpse of their prey. Sands was still behind the machine gun, but he had grown restless after so many hours of sitting still. Canva took his eyes off the woods and glanced at his watch; the guard change would take place in an hour. Everything was going to be okay. Canva radioed Wierzbowski in the chapel. "Wierzbowski, you copy, over?"

"Wierzbowski, over" came the response.

"Any chatter about the hostile, over?"

"Negative, all is quiet, over"

"Roger that, over and out." Well, that brief conversation had told Canva what he needed to know. There had not been any sign of the hostile, but it was still early.

Bridge sat behind the desk in front of the large window, its thick steel bars giving him a sense of security. He sat alone in the dark, his eyes open, his body alert, but his mind resting. It had been a skill he had developed in *Gulf Storm* as a lieutenant. He would maintain consciousness but let his mind rest and refresh itself. He continued the trait to this day. If he allowed himself to fall asleep in the traditional sense, it would take too long for his body to wake up. With the threat they were facing, anything short of an immediate response was insufficient. Yet outside of the window, something prowled, staying outside the range of the sensors that the soldiers had put up, waiting until the time to strike was right.

Canva still stood waiting until it was time to give up his shift. By his count, it would only be another thirty minutes. There seemed to be some scuffling noises coming from above him. Canva looked up into the night sky but could not see anything above the second floor except the glow coming from windows on the third and fourth floors. The floodlights that had been set up around the perimeter had kept the darkness from completely overtaking the men, but it still held heavy in the air. He was probably just hearing one of the sentries moving position. They had posted a two-man team on the roof's observation deck, just in case the thing tried the same trick twice. Canva was certain that at least one of the men would have been able to get a shot off before they would have been attacked.

A large, black shape fell to the ground only a few feet from Canva's position. Sands jumped and squeezed off a quick burst of machine gun rounds into the shape. It made a wet tearing sound as the slugs hit the shape. "Cease fire!" Canva ordered.

He hopped the small sandbag barricade and turned on the flashlight attached to the end of his rifle. There lay the body of a soldier.

It was not clear who it was, but Canva knew where it had come from. He whirled, preparing to fire the M-4 but unable to see any targets. Then, the rattle of small-arms fire came from within the building. "Wierzbowski, patch me through all frequencies" Canva ordered. He waited a moment until he heard the line clear. "This is Lieutenant Canva! We have a man down outside the main entrance and shots fired on the top floor. I want a sit rep immediately. All exterior forces maintain position. This could be a diversion. I repeat, all external forces remain in position. All interior fire teams not guarding checkpoints proceed to top floor for reconnaissance and engagement. This is Canva, out."

He hated not pulling more men to go inside and make sure that a hostile had not infiltrated their current location, but if this was diversion, Canva refused to be caught with his trousers down when the real attack came.

Inside, Bridge snapped to as the first shots rattled from the M-249 outside the door. Then, all was quiet; he waited to see if more shots were fired, and they were, but not from where he expected. The next volley of shots came from four floors above him, not outside. After he heard Canva's orders, he waited to see what the initial report was. At last, he might finally complete this mission.

Jack tensed as he heard the gunfire outside, but then it rattled off just down the hall. Owen, Ameth, and Emera stood around Jack as he listened. There were sounds of a struggle and a few more volleys of fire. Quickly, Jack grabbed the .38, opened the cylinder to check that it was loaded, flipped it closed, and handed it to Owen. "What are you doing?" Emera asked, her eyes wide with fear.

"Owen's going to take you girls down a floor to the checkpoint and then to Ruby's room. Stay there. I'll be along soon as I can." Jack shifted his gaze from Emera to Owen.

Owen gave a nod to Jack. "Wait a minute," Emera started. "You can't stay up here. These men are soldiers, and they can handle this."

A loud terror-filled scream echoed down the hall. Jack looked back at Emera and said, "I don't think they can. I've got to try and help. Now, go with Owen."

Jack opened the door and looked down to the end of their hallway and could see that all the room doors were open, which meant the soldiers must either be on duty or where the action was. Over the sound of gunfire, Jack could hear the stomp of combat boots coming up the stairs from the lower floors. He looked over his shoulder at his friends. "Go."

He went through the double doors into the foyer, where the chapel was. The door had been shut back, most likely with all the communications gear safely locked inside. Jack looked through the round window in the doors to the other hallway and stopped. It was another creature like the one from the night before, but this one had a thicker, longer coat of brown fur. The fur was matted with dark patches of what Jack could only surmise was blood. Soldiers were running toward it, smoke from the rifles filling the hall. To any observer, it appeared to be a chaotic situation; the soldiers were moving in attempting to get clear lines of fire, firing only to be dealt a blow that was leaving behind many injured and dead men. The close quarters were causing more men to be wounded by crossfire and friendly fire, effectively leaving them easy prey for the monster rampaging in the hall.

Owen and the girls followed Jack through the door and caught sight of the monstrosity engaged in battle. "What in God's name?" Ameth started.

"God's got nothing to do with it." Jack replied.

A small group of soldiers came to the top of the stairs and ran past them into the fray on the other side of the double door. There was no sound coming from the stairs anymore. Owen led the girls to the spiral staircase, never turning his back to the double doors. "Jack," Emera called.

He turned toward her, and she threw something to him. Jack caught it. It was the silver chain with the wolf's head pendant. Jack clasped it in his hand. Owen and the girls were going down the stairs, headed toward what Jack could only hope was safety. He looked back in the window and saw that the situation had not improved. He steadied himself and stepped through the doors. The view was far worse on this side of the door. There were bodies lying everywhere. Some of them were wounded and trying to escape the bloodbath that had dominated the hallway. Other bodies were lying in broken heaps. Only three soldiers seemed to be capable of fighting, and Jack knew they were going to need his help. Strewn around the floor were M-4 rifles and the shotguns that the soldiers had carried. Jack picked up the nearest shotgun and found a soldier nearby with shotgun shells slipped into loops on his belt. Jack took several of the shells and made sure that the shotgun was filled to capacity.

He had used shotguns growing up, so he took to this one fairly quickly. The three unscathed soldiers began moving in at a crouch, firing at the ravaging monster that had already dealt with so many other soldiers. Several of the bullets hit their mark, but the beast was quick. It leaped into the nearest room. The soldiers stopped in the hall and froze. Trying to determine their next tactical step was all it took. The beast lunged into the

81

Friedkin's Curse

middle of the hall floor and threw itself at the center soldier, landing on him with its legs preparing to spring again. With the fierce claws adorning its hands, it took a quick swipe on each side and ripped the throat of one soldier while tearing deep gouges into the shoulder of the other one. The arterial spray from the soldier's savaged neck covered the side of the beast's face in a fresh coating of crimson. One deft motion with the left foot, and it had pushed the pinned man's chin to the floor. With a cold and calculating motion, it grabbed his shoulder and twisted in the opposite direction. There was a snap, and the man's body jumped and then all was still. The wounded were crying, and the rest were dying. Jack stood alone in a hallway of mangled men, who had been trained for this, and pumped a shell into the chamber of the shotgun. The beast tore into the meat of the soldier whose neck had just been broken, believing there to be no challenge left. Jack whistled.

The beast stopped mid-bite and looked up at him. Their eyes met, and Jack realized that this beast wanted nothing but murder and mayhem. Those eyes stared at him with nothing but hate burning brightly. Gunfire erupted from the lawn. Jack pulled the shotgun to his shoulder and prepared to fire as the beast came at him on all fours moving incredibly fast. Jack squeezed the trigger and the shot went high. He had not expected the powerful kick of the army's ammunition, not realizing that it was a magnum-caliber shotgun shell. He pumped once, and the beast was on him. One furry, blood covered shoulder of corded muscle drove into him and pushed him against the wall, forcing the wind out of him. The creature let him go and caught him by the throat with a massive hand. Jack could not bring the shotgun up in these confined quarters, and a wild shot would most likely blow the shotgun out of his grasp. He took a swing at the beast, but knew it was fruitless. His vision blurred, and then it dropped him and let out a cry that was a mix between anger and pain.

Jack's vision cleared, and he could see the side of the beast's muzzle smoking, the flesh bubbling as if burned. Looking down, he saw the silver chain and pendant glowing as it dangled from his wrist. It must have made contact with the monster and reacted. Jack did not waste any time. He pulled the shotgun to his shoulder, took aim, and fired. The beast was blown onto its back, a massive, gaping wound in its chest. It still tried to move, even with the blood pouring out of it. To Jack's amazement, the blood began to subside, and the chest wound seemed to be getting smaller. With increasing ferocity and energy, the beast began to sit up. Jack kicked its nose, smashing the back of its head onto the floor with a thump. He fired directly into the face of the beast and was satisfied when he witnessed the magnum slug disintegrate most of the beast's head. Just to be sure, Jack watched for a moment to make sure that it was not regenerating as the chest had done. The blood and brain matter did not seem to be slowing. Jack stepped away and fired twice more into where he thought the heart and lungs would be situated. He then stumbled away from the pile of carnage that was the aftermath of the attack this night and vomited against the wall, afterward taking a deep breath and picking up a radio from one of the fallen soldiers.

He could hear Lt. Canva demanding someone inform him of what was going on; Jack obliged and depressed the button to respond. "Lieutenant, this is Jack Houston. You need to send any medics you have up here. There are a lot of wounded men up here. There's also a lot of dead ones, and one big, hairy thing."

After a moment, Canva came back. "What's the condition of the hostile, over?"

Jack looked at the destroyed creature, which seemed to have lost some of its muscle mass and had taken on a more feminine shape. "It's dead."

"Dead? Who brought it down? I need a full report, over?"

"I'll tell you all about it as soon as you get up here." Jack dropped the handset on the floor and walked back to his room, stopping to retrieve more shotgun shells along the way. The shotgun had been pretty effective against the beast. It may still come in handy, because Jack knew that was not the same beast that had come into the building the night before. The blood and viscera on the bottom of his shoes made a squelching sound as he walked out of the carnage filled hallway. Stowing the shotgun in the room and rinsing off the bottom of his shoes in the bathroom sink, he headed downstairs to join the rest of his group in Ruby's room.

Several different medics passed him on the stairs followed by more soldiers. None of them tried to stop him. He walked past the sentries on the third floor and entered the double doors. Most of the doors were closed, but a few were cracked. He could hear familiar voices coming from one of the rooms halfway down the hall. He knocked and then pushed the door open. Ruby sitting on a lower bunk with another girl on the top, both wearing what appeared to be nightshirts featuring different cartoon characters. Emera and Ameth were sitting beside Ruby. Owen stood next to the bed leaning against it. Jack noticed Owen move his hand from behind his back, most likely reaching for the revolver. Emera's eyes shimmered with the tears she was trying to fight back. Ameth just looked at Jack with an inquisitive look. Ruby, unaware of the danger most likely, just waved at him from the bottom bunk. He winked at her and Emera. "What happened Jack?" Ruby asked.

"Nothing special." He said to Ruby. "What do you think happened?"

She shrugged her shoulders. "I don't know, I thought it was something bad, like maybe the monster came back."

Jack laughed. "Are you kidding me? I scared him away."

The little girl from the top bunk spoke. "I saw him outside."

"When?" Jack asked.

"A little bit ago, the soldiers shot at him. And he went away." She lied down after that.

That explained the shots Jack heard from out front; he reached out his hand to Emera, who took it. Her palms were clammy; they always got that way when she was scared. He helped her off of the bed and led her out of the room. Owen and Ameth followed them out. "Goodnight guys." Ruby said as Ameth pulled the door closed behind them.

Emera could not hold back her tears anymore and began crying. Her body wracked with sobs as she buried her face into Jack's chest. He wrapped his arms around her as she wept. After a few moments, her sobbing became less severe and gradually stopped. Jack let her go, and she looked up at him and kissed him. Her tears added a hint of salt to her kisses. "I was so scared." She said.

"I wouldn't let that thing get down here." He said, rubbing her back.

"Not that," she said. "I was scared you wouldn't be coming back."

The realization that he might have died actually hit him, harder than the dead beast he had left upstairs. His smile faltered and his eyes told that he had just realized his own mortality. "So, what happened?" Owen asked, breaking Jack out of his revelatory daze.

"I've got to meet with one of the higher ups." He shook his head, clearing his mind of the death that he had just faced unaware. "I killed it, but I don't think it was the same one as last night. Do you remember what color it was, Owen?"

"Very dark," Owen said.

"That's what I thought, this one was light brown."

"So what there's more than one?" Ameth said with a tinge of both fear and amazement.

"I guess so." Jack said. "I've got something that seemed to work against it pretty well stashed in the room. That's our secret."

They all nodded their agreement. Whatever their initial thoughts about the military's arrival and their predicament, it had just turned sinister.

Part 3: From Out of the Past

Jack, Owen, Ameth, and Emera returned to the small room and waited. Outside in the hallway, they could hear the soldiers going about cleaning up and tending to the wounded. After a couple of hours had passed, there was a knock on the door. Jack had been expecting it and opened the door. It was Canva. "The General would like to have a word with you." It was not a request.

Jack looked back at his companions and gave a short wave. He stepped out into the hall and closed the door behind him. As he followed the large Hawaiian down the hall and past the double doors into the foyer, where the chapel was, Jack could see that the men were still cleaning, but it looked as if the dead and wounded had been moved. Down the stairs they went, the soldier with his M-4 slung across his shoulders, Jack with his hands in his pockets. Canva opened the door to what had been Ms. Toews office and stepped aside to allow Jack to enter, afterwards closing the door and remaining outside. It was Bridge and Jack, a few chairs and a desk between them. Bridge held out his hand toward one of the chairs. They both sat at the same time, never breaking eye contact.

Finally, after a few tense seconds, Bridge spoke. "I understand you were able to assist my men."

"I'm not sure how much assisting I did. It was more like saving from where I was standing." Jack's anger at Bridge was growing. The man had known the dangers and had still insisted they stay there.

"Whate'er the case, my men and I wish to thank you." Bridge struck a match to light his cigar. "But rest assured, I don't think we'll need your assistance any more."

Friedkin's Curse

"We both know that wasn't the one you're here for."

This caught Bridge off guard, his match hovering near the tip of his cigar. He instead shook out the match and laid the cigar on the desk. Jack could clearly see the contempt this man had for him. "You don't know half as much as you think you do."

"Then, teach me. What is going on here? And what was that thing decimating your men upstairs?"

"That thing, the thing you just happened to kill. Well, when my men were cleaning up,, they found a nude, Caucasian female missing most of her face and a large chunk of tit. We believe it's Samantha Croul. She's the only person unaccounted for." Bridge smiled at him, a malicious grin that spread across his face. "So tell me, what was that thing upstairs decimating my men?"

"It wasn't Samantha when I shot it, and it sure as hell wasn't Samantha when it was tearing your men apart." You know what it is, Jack thought before he voiced. "You're hunting a werewolf." Jack couldn't believe the words coming out of his mouth, but there was no other logical explanation, the transformation, the reaction to the silver pendant. What else could it have been?

"How am I supposed to answer that?"

"It wasn't a question, General. Your men were too well equipped to not know what they were dealing with. How long have you been tracking this thing?"

"Any information regarding military operations is strictly classified and cannot be discussed with civilians. If we request your assistance, we'll debrief you and not before."

"It's weapons, isn't it? You want to harness it to be a living weapon. Of course, drop it on a battlefield and let it wreak havoc. I can't believe I'm saying this, but Jesus, this is a bad movie plot."

"I suggest you go back to your quarters. Meals will be brought up later." Bridge ended the conversation by spinning the chair away from Jack and facing toward the window.

Jack stepped out of the office and found Canva waiting for him. Canva followed him up the stairs and stood at the double doors, watching as Jack entered the room and closed the door behind him. He picked up the old, worn journal of General Friedkin.

His friends asked him what had happened, and he told them of his conversation with Bridge and of his own suspicions. The night was broken by the sound of a helicopter. Judging by the sound, Owen and Jack assumed it was flying too low to be commercial. Looking out the window, they saw a large helicopter, which Jack thought was a Chinook. With a large rotor in front and back, it set down, the winds produced by the rotors blowing through the darkened woods and bending back the trees. The rotors slowed and then stopped.

One of the large trucks the soldiers had rode into the school on was driving toward it. Brake lights flared as the truck pulled alongside the large helicopter. A ramp in the rear lowered.

"What do you think it is?" Emera asked.

"Wounded maybe." Owen offered.

"No, look." Ameth pointed as several soldiers came down the ramp and started pulling long, black, vinyl bags out of the rear of the truck.

Jack watched as they made trip after trip, carrying the bags from the truck into the back of the helicopter. His mind was lost with what he was seeing and what he had witnessed earlier in the hall. "That's too many."

"What?" Emera asked.

"That's too many." Jack's mind raced over the sights he had seen earlier. "There weren't that many dead men and not all of the wounds were fatal." He snapped his fingers. "They killed them."

Owen turned from the window. "Who killed who?"

"Follow me. The wounded had been bitten and clawed by a werewolf, which will cause them to then become werewolves. To keep them from turning, they were executed. Bridge killed his own men."

"Why didn't he kill you?" Owen asked.

Jack thought for a minute. "It didn't wound me."

Jack sat down, and Emera sat beside him and slipped her hand in his. He gave it a light squeeze. Ameth made her way back to the bed, while Owen watched until the last of the bodies had been transferred. As Owen turned from the window the large engines on the helicopter began to whine and then smooth out as they warmed, finally fading as the helicopter left to take the bodies to their final destination.

Owen and Ameth slept curled together. Emera was lying with her head in Jack's lap. He stroked her hair until her breathing eased and she slept. Jack looked out the window and waited for the dawn to come. Until then, he'd have to hope he could find some answers in the journal. He opened the book and began reading.

Bridge sat with his eyes open, letting his mind rest but pondering over the revelation. The teacher Croul had been turned before their arrival. It had to have happened during the beast's initial visit to the school. He was not sure how. No one had reported any injury during the incident and no medical personnel had been requested. A key to the puzzle lay in the answer to that question: how did she get infected?

Bridge thought about the men who had been wounded. It was a shame. They were all fine soldiers, but the orders were clear: any contamination must be exterminated. Only two of the soldiers who had been in the fray had survived without infectious wounds, the two he had reprimanded earlier, Jonas and Wickes. They were lucky. According to their statement, Jonas had opened the door at the first gunshot and when he did, he was kicked or tossed - Jonas could not remember which - into the room, becoming a human projectile that had landed on Wickes, who had just returned from the kitchen, and knocked them both unconscious. Jonas had severely bruised ribs according to the medic, but nothing that would have allowed for the spread of the disease.

The sun rose above the trees and cast a golden glow over the school grounds. Even the bright golden rays could not penetrate all the way through the depth of the forest. The shadows remained and held their secrets. Shining through the window on the fourth floor, Emera was the first to stir as the rays caressed her cheek and roused her from her slumber. Her head was still in Jack's lap. He was sitting against the headboard as he had been last night. A book lay on his other leg, and his head hung forward, almost resting on his chest. His chest was gently rising as Emera sat up. The slight movement instantly woke Jack. "It's okay." She said, resting her hand on his shoulder.

He took several quick blinks, clearing the sleep from his eyes and the fog from his mind. He had been reading the journal when he'd fallen asleep. Judging by the crick in his neck, he'd slept several hours. Owen sat up and looked at them. Ameth opened her eyes and grimaced, rolled over and tried to go back to sleep.

There was a knock at the door. Owen looked at his watch and then at the door. Being closest, he rolled off of the small mattress and opened it. There was a soldier at the door, who said something in a muffled voice to Owen and walked down the hall. Closing the door, Owen turned back to the others. "He says that breakfast will be available in a few minutes in the dining room."

They left the room together as the soldiers watched them with interest, Owen and Jack not trusting the men, given what had occurred shortly after the soldiers arrived; most, however, were trying to get a look at Jack, the man who had stopped one of the monsters they were hunting. The sentries at every floor were looking the quartet over. No one spoke to them until they reached the dining hall. There Ruby and some of her friends were quite talkative: wanting to know what had happened the night before, if the soldiers seemed nice, and wondering where Ms. Croul was. Jack couldn't tell them. It would be known soon enough. He looked around and saw Simone sitting with another group of students at the table she had been sitting at their first evening here. She was obviously haggard and worn; he suspected that she had been informed of her colleague's demise. Jack hated that he had done it, but it had needed to be done. He had no other choice.

There were a few small groups of soldiers sitting on the opposite end of the dining room from the others. They were eating, smoking, and talking. Jack gave them a quick glance and saw the two that had given them the trouble earlier. The men returned Jack's gaze. Jack sat down next to Emera, but never broke eye contact with Jonas. Finally, Jonas looked at one of the other soldiers, and Jack smiled and returned his attention to the people around him. Ruby was in her school uniform without the blazer; Jack noticed that most of the children in fact weren't wearing theirs. "The soldiers let us cook just like always and even asked if we could make extra for them." Ruby was smiling with pride at having been asked to cook for the soldiers.

"That's good," Emera said. "So, what else have the soldier's done?" Emera's face did not betray her hidden concerns; after everything that had happened and with what Jack had told them about his theories, she was concerned for her sister's safety. Not just from the monsters in the woods, but the monsters roaming the halls in uniform.

"One of them showed us how to tell who was in charge by the stripes on their sleeves." Ruby took a big bite of scrambled eggs. With her mouth half-full, she continued. "It was pretty cool."

"Rube," Ameth said using her nickname, "don't trust these guys. They're not all that nice."

Ameth was talking to Ruby but looking down the table past Jack. He knew who she was looking at. Ruby swallowed her eggs and took a sip of orange juice from her glass. "I know that. What do you think?" She asked looking at her oldest sister's husband.

"Well, I think they are going to protect us, but your sister's right. We don't know these guys, and we never completely trust a stranger, right?"

Ruby nodded her consent to what Owen had said. "Jack?" She asked. He raised an eyebrow at her. "What do you think about them?"

His lips curled up into a smirk. "I think some of them are good and some of them are bad, and I don't want to find out which ones are which. So, for me, I'm going to try and keep a low profile."

Ruby's roommate giggled beside her. "Good luck. I heard some of them say you killed a monster."

Ruby's eyes lit up, and Emera and Ameth both gave him a look which needed no explanation. "Not me, I just stayed upstairs and helped the soldiers a little; I barely did anything." Jack put his elbows on the table and clenched his fist, causing the joints of his hand to pop loudly. "Besides, I'm no soldier. What could I possibly do that these guys couldn't?"

Ruby's roommate thought about it for a minute and then came to the conclusion that Jack was right; he couldn't do anything that the soldiers couldn't. The weight of the pendant was comforting around his wrist as he thought about the encounter the night before and how had it not been for that pendant buying him a fraction of a second, he'd be long dead.

He took the pendant and its chain out from around his wrist and handed it to Emera. "Jack, what's...?"

"Please take it." He said as she closed her hand around it.

She looked at her closed hand and then at Jack. He simply smiled and winked at her. She wasn't sure why he wanted her to have that hideous pendant, but she'd keep it. Besides, it was better than the scary crucifix in the chapel. Jack's eyes glazed over for a second, and Emera shook his knee. He looked at her and smiled. "Still need a little sleep, I guess." He said as he stretched. "Oh, babe, do me a favor stay with Owen or some of the students. I'd rather you not be by yourself." He tilted his head toward the end of the table where the soldiers sat.

She nodded her agreement, and Jack headed back upstairs to the room for some sleep. He'd try to get a little bit more sleep and then get up and read. The door closed behind him, and the soldiers were obviously interested in him. He had stepped up and done what their brothers-in-arms couldn't do. It created a rivalry between him and some of the other soldiers, while in others, it created a sense of camaraderie.

Breakfast lasted a little longer, and then the girls were cleaning up the dishes, taking care of the soldiers first. The soldiers thanked the girls and then left. Jonas and Wickes were giving hard stares at the women they had been denied before, and in their minds, plans began to form. Owen looked around and didn't see Simone anywhere. "Where's the other teacher?" He asked Ameth.

She looked over her shoulder at the table where the last remaining member of staff had been sitting. She shrugged her shoulders and went back to talking with one of the girls nearby. Owen stood up and started to walk back to the kitchen. He heard Ameth clear her throat. Turning, he was more than prepared for the questioning look she was giving him. "I'm going to see where she is. I'd just like to make sure everybody stays safe." He turned back toward his destination and went toward the kitchen.

He opened the door and saw that while several of the girls were still bringing dishes back to be washed, some of the girls had already donned aprons and yellow gloves to wash and dry the dishes. He looked around and still couldn't see Simone.

He walked to the door in the rear of the kitchen, the one he and Jack had chased the monstrosity through. He pushed it open carefully, just in case someone was coming down the hall, he didn't want to hit them with the door. Good thing too. He stopped when he heard the boots coming his way. A small contingent of soldiers headed toward the door and into the warm sunlight. As the door closed behind them, and Owen pushed open the door and stepped into the hallway, he noticed that there was a definite gloom over the hall as opposed to the bright freshness of the outdoors.

95
Friedkin's Curse

Simone was not in the hall. Stepping lightly on the hardwood, Owen was headed toward the study where they had taken tea only two days before. He passed the doorway to the cellar, and as he stepped past it, a hand came to rest on his shoulder. "Shit!" He said as he jumped.

Turning, he saw Simone holding a few jars of what looked like homemade jams and preserves. He could feel the heat creeping up into his face as he blushed over his temporary fright. Simone looked just as startled as him. "I'm so sorry to scare you." She apologized. "I noticed that we were running low on the preserves and thought I'd also get some of our jam for the girls to have for sandwiches at lunch."

Owen's heart began slowing finally; the sudden rush of adrenaline had caused a tremor in his hands. "It's all right. We noticed that you weren't in the room anymore and with some of these soldiers... I just wanted to make sure you're okay."

"Right as rain." She said smiling.

Her complexion seemed a little bit paler than it had before, but that could have been from the mutual fright she and Owen had shared. He escorted her back to the kitchen and then went out into the dining room. Ameth was missing, but Emera still sat at the table talking to Ruby. Owen sat down, watching the doors and waiting on his wife to return. One of the doors opened and Ameth came in. "Well?" She asked.

"She was getting preserves and jam out of the cellar." He explained. "Where were you?"

"Had to go to the little girls' room."

Owen left the sisters together in Ruby's room and proceeded to the ground floor where he headed out into the back of the school. He found a garden of some sort. Large strawberries, raspberries, and apricots were growing. He picked one of the strawberries as he walked by and took a bite. It was plump and juicy. As he let the sweet taste draw him back to his childhood and his grandfather's backyard garden, a smell invaded his nostrils. It brought him from his revelry back to the danger that stalked the woods. He had wandered past the berries and was now among roses and lilies. Still, the smell that had hit him was not a good one. He took a deep whiff and found where the smell was coming from, the nearest row of rose bushes. He knelt and took a look under the bushes. The bile rose in his throat and he vomited into one of the lilies nearby. It took several deep breathes to calm him down and steel his nerves. Another quick glance confirmed what he had thought he saw. It was the severed hand of a man tossed from one of the dead sentries that had been stationed on the roof the night before.

"Sir?" Owen looked up and saw a soldier nearby, looking at him strangely. He was carrying the M-4 in a casual manner that would allow for him to aim and fire within a fraction of a second.

Motioning him closer, Owen pointed under the bush to his grisly discovery. The soldier saw it and radioed for assistance. Had the soldier not been patrolling and stumbled across him, he was not sure what he would have done next. His legs were unsteady as he stood and began leaving the garden, the thought to look back did not once enter his mind. The only thing he needed was to get away from the sickeningly sweet mixture of roses, lilies, and decaying flesh. His mouth was awash with the horrid sweetness of the strawberry and the acidic bitter of bile. He wanted to be somewhere inside, so he could get a cold glass of water or something else to wash the taste out of his mouth.

The alarm on Jack's cell phone went off, and he sat up and checked the time. Two hours had passed since he came upstairs and laid down. Emera and Ameth were nowhere to be seen, and Owen was sitting on the other bed looking sick. "Where are the girls?" Jack asked.

"They went to stay with Ruby. We'll see them at lunch." Owen took a sip of bottled water.

"What happened to you?"

"I went for a walk in the garden." Owen's eyes locked on Jack's face. As if staring past him, Owen recounted the discovery he had made.

After Owen finished, Jack sat silent. Owen turned and stared out the window, not really focusing on anything. Jack sat up on the bed and opened the journal of General Friedkin. He began to skim the pages, stopping when he came to a bit of information he felt might be useful. In his scavenging for information, he had yet to discover anything of any value relating to the estate. It was predominantly his accounts of his time in service. Diligently, Jack continued turning the pages, searching for any assistance from out of the past and yet, careful of the old, delicate pages beneath his fingertips. Owen lapsed into sleep while sitting up. Jack looked up from the journal when there was a loud knock on the door; Owen's head jerked with a start as he realized that he had fallen asleep. The soldier at the door informed them that it was time for lunch.

The students were coming out of their rooms as Jack and Owen reached their floor. At this point, they both recognized the majority of the girls. They saw Ruby but not her sisters. Jack knelt to get on her level. "Where's Emera and Ameth?"

"One of the soldiers asked them to help with lunch in the kitchen." Ruby said, looking at Jack puzzled.

"Thanks. We'll see you down there." Jack said as he and Owen began walking faster down the stairs, weaving their way past students. Once they were clear of the students, their walk became a run.

Jack and Owen were both thinking the worst, given their initial encounter with the soldiers. They opened the doors and saw that the tables were set, but there wasn't any food on the tables. The far door of the kitchen seemed miles away as they both sprinted across the dining room, pushing open the door. The startled expressions on the faces of the women and girls were obvious signs that everything had been okay. Jack put his hands on his head as he stepped back out into the dining room. He took a deep breath trying to calm his body. Every muscle in his body was aching as the adrenaline his body had released in anticipation of a fight coursed through him. Owen was fidgeting with his hands and fingers, obviously trying to expel some of his own nervous energy. As the door to the kitchen had opened, they both knew they had been wrong. Their female companions were safe. They had been standing around a large, metal table with Simone and several of the students, preparing sandwiches. Peanut butter and jelly was one of the options, and it appeared some kind of lunch meat, ham most likely, given the pink hue of the meat.

Ameth and Emera came out behind the guys. Emera put her hand on Jack's shaking shoulder while Ameth stood with her arms crossed waiting for an explanation. "You okay?" Emera asked.

Jack just shook his head. Ameth stood looking at Owen, not asking any questions. Owen did have one question, though. "Why didn't you stay in Ruby's room?"

"They came and asked if we could help make lunch." Emera explained.

"Not as if two members of the faculty are missing." Ameth snipped. "We're adults, boys. Try to remember that."

"Did you forget the two soldiers we met? The ones who tried to take our room, and you girls." Owen said, taking a deep breath.

Ameth opened her mouth to continue the argument but closed it right back as the door to the dining hall opened, and the students began to come in. Ameth turned and went back into the kitchen. The attitude she was conveying with her body language let Owen know that this discussion would be picked up later. Emera kissed Jack on the cheek and whispered into his ear. "Sorry to worry you."

"It's cool." He said as she went back to the kitchen also.

After the meal was over, Emera and Ameth began to help Simone and several of the students carry the dirty dishes back into the kitchen. The remaining students headed out of the dining hall and back up the stairs to their rooms. *Kids are probably going stir crazy,* Jack thought. He and Owen had decided they would wait until the girls were done and then they'd go back upstairs to the room together.

Jonas and Wickes waited outside the dining room, standing to the side. They had not seen the guys come out yet, which was fine with Jonas. He wanted a rematch with Jack. This time, he was ready; no cheap-shot head butts would put him down. The thought of it made him angry. His nose and sinuses throbbed whenever he lay down to try and get some sleep. In his mind, he saw the payback he'd inflict on Jack. He'd cut him with his combat knife, really hurt him good, take the fight out of him, and then get to know his lady friend. It was a thought that made Jonas smile, one fueled by malice and cruelty, but it was a smile nonetheless.

Ameth and Emera came out of the dining room door, Jack and Owen following close behind them. They all saw Jonas and Wickes. The girls quickened their pace toward the stairs. Jack and Owen matched their pace to keep up. "Hey, big' un!" Jonas called.

Jack stopped on the first step and turned around. Owen did, too. The girls just stood rooted to the spot.

"We'll meet you in the room." Owen said.

"Go on up, it'll all be fine." Jack said. When he saw them start back up the stairs, he was able to focus fully on the man in front of him.

"Glad you let the ladies leave." Jonas put his hand on Jack's shoulder and gave a slight push. "Didn't want them to see you get your ass handed to you, eh?"

Jack did not say anything. He merely met Jonas' stare. Wickes and Owen had subconsciously distanced themselves from their larger counterparts. The anger was coming off of Jonas in waves. Jack remained calm, his jaw set.

"I'm talking to you, asshole." Jonas said as he put his hand on Jack's shoulder again. "What are you going to . . .?" Jonas finished his sentence with a yelp.

Jack had grabbed Jonas' hand and twisted the limb around into a wrist lock. Jonas reached with his free hand to retrieve his knife from his boot. It was almost completely free when Jack wretched up the pressure on his wrist. The sudden spasm of pain caused his grip to falter and the knife dropped to the floor. The three remaining men looked at it as Jonas felt the tendons in his wrist drawing tight, near the point of tearing. Jack stared at the knife longer than the others. Wickes had begun to make his way toward the small side hallway that would take him outside. "Wait a minute," Jack said.

Friedkin's Curse

Something in his voice made Wickes stop still. Fear crossed his face. Where Jonas was a lion, it was obvious that Wickes was a vulture. He got the scraps from his friend's feasts. With Jonas firmly in the wrist lock and doubled over at the waist, Jack kicked him in the back of the knee, causing him to fall and in one fluid motion jerked his arm, forcing him to turn halfway around. As his knees connected with the floor, Jack laid his large left hand into Jonas' jaw. The big man's head jerked in reaction to the massive blow, and his body fell backwards. He was awake, but he did not know where he was. "Help your friend, and tell him next time I won't be so forgiving for trying to pull a knife on me." Wickes nodded as he ran over to his friend and tried to help him up.

Jack and Owen began up the stairs, with the sound of Wickes' struggling fading behind them. "Where did you learn that stuff?" Owen asked.

"I used to get picked on as a kid." Jack said, smiling. "My mom signed me up for a self-defense class at the Y. My uncle was a Marine and he taught me some stuff, then in college, all my electives were the martial arts P.E. classes. I think he was trying to lure me into a fight so he could kill me."

"Seems that way." Owen agreed.

They caught up with the girls at the top of the third flight of stairs. Ameth and Emera were waiting for them, it seemed. Together, they went to their room.

Jack sat down with the book once again and opened it while the others talked and rested. To any outside observer, it would have been obvious the stress of the situation was beginning to wear on them. Exhaustion seemed to come upon them easier as the strain of the tension grew. Between the monsters outside and the soldiers inside, it seemed that no matter which way they turned, there was no ally, only enemies and obstacles.

Before the sun began its descent into the west and the night closed in around the isolated estate, a soldier came and asked if Ameth and Emera would mind assisting with the preparation of dinner. They agreed, and Jack and Owen escorted them down to the kitchen. Once they saw that the girls were safely with Simone and the students helping cook, they went out the large double doors in the front and saw the soldiers standing at the ready. It was noticeably darker down here than on their room on the fourth floor. Jack noticed the soldier at the bottom of the steps nestled behind his M-249 machine gun, and a man sticking out of the roof hatch of a nearby Humvee poised and ready behind a .50 caliber mounted machine gun. If the rest of the place was as heavily guarded and well-armed as the front, then it would not be an easy task for anything to get into the building now. With Samantha's death and all the wounded soldiers "evacuated" according to General Bridge, the only real concern was the beast still at large. There had been no further invasions by the beast and hopefully no other surprises. It was steadily getting darker, and crickets were chirping from the lawn. Owen and Jack headed back in and went upstairs to their room. Jack put the .38 in the waist of his jeans, near his hip. Just in case, he thought to himself as he felt the reassuring weight pulling down his jeans. Tightening his belt another notch, he looked at Owen, who nodded.

"You know, I'm really sick and tired of these stairs." Owen said as they once again came to the landing.

"An elevator would be nice," Jack agreed.

There was a burst of static from the nearby chapel. Jack and Owen went to see what equipment Wierzbowski had. It was possible that they may be able to get a call out to someone who could assist them. Neither man voiced the idea, but they were both thinking it. Stepping around to the door, they knocked and then pushed the door open and looked in. Wierzbowski was facing away from them as static rose from one of the nearby machines. Owen inched toward Wierzbowski, Jack coming up beside Owen, his hand on the butt of the revolver. Owen reached out and lightly tapped Wierzbowski on the shoulder. The man spun around and reached for his pistol. Both Owen and Jack raised their hands. The communication's officer looked from one to the other and started laughing. He put the headphones around his neck. "Sorry, guys, it gets lonely, and I didn't realize I had company."

"It's all right." Owen said. "Didn't mean to sneak up on you. We knocked, and you didn't really respond."

"It's the job, some of it's very detail-oriented, and I tend to get lost in it. Hope I didn't scare you guys."

They both assured the soldier that they were fine and went back down the stairs to the dining hall. Both men walked through the dining hall and peeked in the kitchen. Emera was stirring a pot of something that made the men's mouths salivate when the aroma reached their nostrils. Owen looked around and once again did not see his wife. "Emera, where did my better half get off to this time?"

Emera looked up from the pot and smiled at them. "She went to the cellar to help Simone carry up some things."

Owen considered going to help, but before he had made a decision Ameth came in the kitchen carrying several large potatoes. Simone was not with her. "I'm back." She proclaimed to the kitchen helpers. Owen thought she was favoring her right leg, walking with a slight limp.

She stopped laughing when she saw Jack and Owen standing in the doorway. She winked at Owen. He just smiled and turned to go back to the dining room. Jack followed him. "Was that odd?" Jack asked.

"What?" Owen asked.

"Well, I've known you guys a while, and I've never seen Ameth wink at you. What's up with that?"

"She occasionally surprises me, too." Owen said with a suggestive nudge of Jack's elbow.

"Oh," Jack said, thinking about the statement, and then thought to himself that Owen would most likely know his wife better than Jack did.

They sat down at the table they had occupied previously and waited for the students to come down for their meals. The girls arrived as one big group talking with one another. They were talking so fast that Jack and Owen did good to pick out a word or two from the conversations. Ruby sat where she had sat previously, but her friend was not with her. "Where's your friend?" Jack asked.

"She's not feeling good." Ruby said, leaning across the table Ruby whispered. "Her stomach gets real upset when she gets stressed. I'm going to try and sneak her a glass of milk. She's been complaining ever since lunch." Ruby winked at the men.

Jack and Owen couldn't help but smile at the innocent gesture, as if Ruby thought she was planning a bank robbery. No soldiers joined them for the meal. When they left the dining hall, there were no soldiers outside the door. They could hear the sounds of movement outside and orders being shouted. It was apparent that the soldiers were expecting more company tonight. With the soldiers preoccupied, Jack and Owen felt safe leaving Ameth and Emera with Ruby to spend some time and say goodnight.

As they started up the stairs, Jack asked Owen a simple question. "You feel like doing some reading?"

"Of what?" He responded.

Jack reminded Owen of the journals that Ms. Toews had given him. Once they reached their rooms, Owen began working on the journal from the tobacco farmer while Jack went back to General Friedkin's journal.

While Jack and Owen were engrossed in their reading, sitting below them in the same Humvee that had taken Ms. Toews to her final resting place were Jones and Royston. Jones was sitting in his perch, hands resting on top of the Humvee. His .50 caliber machine gun was ready to fire at a moment's notice. Until that moment arrived, he was relaxing, waiting for the coming battle when he could deal out death in a white-hot blaze of gunfire. He took a drag off of his lit cigarette, letting the acrid smoke burn in his lungs before exhaling. His mind would often drift during the downtime, mainly to the first time he had used the .50. His eyes had lit up like a kid on Christmas at the raw power of the gun, the destruction that stood as a testament to Jones having been there leaving in him a deep sense of satisfaction. It was a decisive moment in his life, the moment he knew he was meant to be a soldier. Sitting inside the Humvee leaning against the passenger's side door with his feet stretched out on the bench seat was Royston.

Royston was writing a letter to his Aunt Deirdre as he did every week. After his parents had died, his aunt had taken him in and raised him. He felt bad that he had to lie to her every week, but the mission was classified. If he tried to tell her, and the brass found out, he'd be in one of the less-desirable details. Given everything he had witnessed Bridge do, he thought it more likely that he'd end up dead. It didn't bother him; he simply told Aunt Deirdre that he had been stationed in Germany. It was the truth; he had been stationed in Germany, but after his scores on the road courses, General Bridge had personally selected him to be his driver. It was an exciting detail, just as Bridge had said it would be, but after watching so many men die horribly, he longed to go back to a simpler life in the barracks or as a civilian. Once this hitch was over, that was what he planned to do.

Canva stood on the front steps of the school and scanned the darkness with a pair of night-vision binoculars. The lights would be on soon, but until then the darkness encroaching on the school held great danger that could spring on them at any time. Canva thought over the men that had served with him just over the course of the assignment. He had seen so many die, ripped apart. For him, capturing the beast had become a part of who he was. He wanted to know that the men, his men had not died in vain. With the night approaching, the chill wind came, which Canva had never gotten used to. It had been fourteen years since he had left Hawaii and its mild, tropical temperature and gentle ocean breezes still haunted him and called to him. He did not let his mind stay on his native home for long. Deep inside, he knew that when his guard was down, he was more likely to end up like his predecessor: dead and buried.

Bridge sat at the desk, chewing on the end of a cigar that was no longer lit. He didn't notice. His mind was occupied with the battle ahead and the thoughts of what he might actually be close to accomplishing. Jack, the interloper as Bridge tended to think of him, had deduced what they were after and some of the why, but he still had far too few of the

107
Friedkin's Curse

pieces to know what true evil this monstrosity was capable of inflicting. With Bridge at the post and his men in position, they were finally one step ahead; they wouldn't be cleaning up after the beast. Samantha Croul had been an acceptable loss; it was the least collateral damage that they'd incurred at the hands of the beast since he first began the hunt. Pack after pack of these monsters had been laid low under Bridge's boot heel, only the alpha male escaping each time. It was finally time to turn the tables on him.

Jonas and Wickes were patrolling the perimeter, staying somewhat alert while they grumbled to each other. Jonas about how he couldn't wait to meet back up with that guy. "No knife for me next time, just one bullet right to the brain. POW!" Jonas exclaimed, finishing his rant and startling Wilkes.

"I just wanted some female companionship." He was saying as he sulked along beside Jonas.

"Once I'm finally done with the big one, his friend won't be a problem for the two of us. Then, well, you know the rest, Wilkes." They both smiled at the prurient thoughts that glided into their minds and displayed not the women they were after, but the women they had already caught and the horrors they had put them through.

Unaware of all the different thoughts and dangers on the ground outside, Jack and Owen continued to read. After several pages, Jack finally came to Friedkin's first entries involving the land.

May 10, 1865 – Found the town of Mead's Hall today. Its citizenry is fair of skin and hair and seem to be of Nordic descent. They are a good people but seemed rather superstitious with charms hanging about their houses. A day's ride to the West and I have found the land where I will bring Gloria and Abigail to start our life afresh. It is a plush land. I must enquire of the government and seek if any man owns this land.

Jack skimmed through the next few entries as they detailed how Friedkin had purchased the land from the government. Then, the process by which the supplies had been brought to the site and the hiring of the workers. Then from the yellowed pages came another clue, this one involving the cellar.

July 14, 1865 – While the workers were excavating the area that will be our root cellar, they struck upon a curious thing. Apparently, an underground cavern traverses the site of my intended home. The workers removed the space for the foundation and the root cellar, yet the cavern entrance entices me. At dawn, I shall depart into the cave with the first early morning light. I must not make a full day of it, as Gloria and lovely Abigail will be joining me on tomorrow evening if their travel arrangements have not altered.

Jack saw the next page and then checked to make sure that no pages were missing, as the dates were off by several days.

July 18, 1865 – After my ordeal in the wilderness, it is good to be back in the comforts of modernity with family. Gloria had been upset when she arrived and found that I had gone missing. I had followed the cavern for several hours. The rock formations are breathtaking, and the environment is like entering an alien terrain from one of Verne's tales. After checking my pocket watch and seeing how the time had passed me, I attempted to make my way back only then realizing that the cavern was part of a larger system. Labyrinthine passages made it impossible to tell from whence I had originally breached that underworld. I finally came to an opening in the earth and climbed out of the natural maze that had confounded me so greatly. I found myself in the woods, and the sun had taken its leave for the day. I was not sure how much oil my lamp possessed and made my way to the largest tree I could find. It was a fine sturdy oak. I slept that night on the second branch, which was high enough for me to climb to.

When the sun rose into the sky, I awoke as its rays touched my face. Attempting to get my bearings, I made my way in the direction I believed would lead me back to the construction underway. I walked for most of the day, not taking care for food or water. The sun once again began its repose, and I knew I would not find rescue until the next day. Taking solace in a tree again, I was relieved to see the moon with its bright face cast light over the forest. My thirst had become so great from my exertions of the day that I left my perch and began to search for water. I could find no fruit or water supply within my immediate vicinity. Therefore, I wandered throughout, until I came to a rocky outcropping in a small clearing. Near the rocks, I found a dip in the earth that had filled with water. I drank greedily until the water was almost done for. Upon second glance, I learned that the dip I thought I was drinking from was actually the paw print of an animal. I could not say certainly, but I believe it to have been the paw print of a wolf of some sort. I took solace among the rocks that night and slept in a nook under one of them.

Upon waking, I felt reinvigorated and set off on my quest home with a new zeal. The path to my destination was simple for me to find; it may seem ludicrous but I felt that I could smell the lavender bath salt that Gloria uses, and following that source, I stepped out of the forest into the land that had been cleared to build my home. I saw that the workers had not stopped in my absence and the construction continued on unabated. Gloria and Abigail were in my tent, no doubt troubled by my absence. I was greeted with many warm embraces and tender kisses by them both when I stepped inside.

July 19, 1865 – Apparently, there was some commotion last night. One of the workers is missing and his tent and living quarters are in shambles. It appears that a wild beast took the man into the forest. I fear for Abigail and Gloria's safety. I will send them into town. The men are drawing straws to stand watch. No one seems to have seen or heard anything, but one of the men confided in me that he thought he heard something being dragged into the woods. A search of the surrounding area has yet to reveal the missing man. I've noticed that some of the men reek from the work they've been doing and the lack of showering facilities. It smells like rain today, so hopefully some of them will bathe.

July 20, 1865 – They have spotted it! The men on watch last night spotted a large beast prowling the grounds around two o'clock; the clouds parted and allowed enough moonlight to see by, and they spotted it searching through the camp. Both men were able to fire their weapons and drive the beast back into the woods. One of the men is confident that he was able to deal a mortal wound to the creature. I do hope so.

I find myself weary and haggard. Despite sleeping soundly the past two nights, it feels as if I have not rested for days. I pray that my exposure on the previous nights did not cause an illness to lodge within. If

111
Friedkin's Curse

I can rest no better for the next few days, I fear I will have to make the trip back to New York and visit Dr. Hawthorne. Today, the workers have started laying the frame for what will be the first level of the house. She'll be four stories when finished, a beauty amongst the trees.

July 21, 1865 – They must have done it; last night, there were no disturbances among the camp. So, the men are stepping more lively, believing the beast dead or frightened away, and I share in their happiness. Despite the peacefulness of the camp, I was plagued in my sleep with visions of horror that drive rest from me and force me to walk about during the day while I miss the covers of the bed within my tent. Perhaps I can rest tonight. I must stay at least until the men are further along, so that Abigail and Gloria may move into their new home.

July 24, 1865 – The masons have begun their work, laying the brick on the exterior of the first floor; the workers have built three floors of the skeleton and should be finished by the end of the month. The interior work has begun as well. I trust that Abigail and Gloria will be able to move in by the middle of August. I miss them dearly, but find my thoughts muddled and confused. My joy at watching the house be erected is overshadowed by the restless nights that plague me and the strange yearnings I feel.

Jack skimmed the next few entries detailing the further building of the house and Friedkin's insomnia. Then, his family moved into the house with a few servants that they brought with them. It was the middle of the month, and Friedkin left for New York to visit his physician about the insomnia and nightmares that caused it.

August 16, 1865 – The good doctor has given me a sleeping tonic to take nightly. I trust that it will assist me in my quest for peace and rest. Last night was the worst by far; the dreams I had were so vivid. I dreamt that I was running through the alleys and backstreets of the city. Nevertheless, I trust tonight I can find solace in my sleep.

August 17, 1865 – My sleep was again restless, even with the tonic that I took. Perhaps it takes more than a night for it to acclimate to my system. I shall try again, and if it does not work tonight ,I shall seek further medical assistance. It seems the city is having its own troubles. The papers report that over the past two nights there have been several connected deaths, all vicious and thought by some to be the work of an animal while others claim a madman. Either one is reason enough for me to want to leave this city for my new home in the country, although I must admit the view of the city under the moonlight is still an enthralling sight.

August 18, 1865 – I had to return to the doctor for more assistance, as his previous tonic did nothing to assist me in obtaining more rest and sleep during the night. The front page of the paper tells of more deaths on the previous evening. Nonetheless, I will be leaving this city on the evening train and arriving at my home sometime tomorrow afternoon. It appears I will be forced to lodge at the local tavern in Mead's Hall this night before proceeding home. At least the moon will light the landscape for me.

August 19, 1865 – I sit awaiting my breakfast, although I am not hungry and feel angry at my lack of rest. Something seems to have put the villagers on edge; the women are going about, squawking like chickens while their men are going about nailing shutters closed and putting thicker doors up. I don't understand the language they are speaking, but it sounds similar to the German I heard used by certain Pennsylvanian people.

Upon request, the bartender told me that a great beast was seen in the village the night before. "A demon from the old world," he said. I wanted to laugh at their superstition, but then it froze in my throat as I remembered the men talking about the beast in their camp. Perhaps they had not wounded it but merely frightened it into the village. I immediately made my way to the small wire station in the village and sent a telegram to a friend from my bloodier days with the Union. I had met a man, a great hunter from Vermont. His boast was that there was no beast he could not hunt and kill, claimed to be part Indian. I am requesting his help and told him that reports of the beast were during the full lunar activity, but it may be active other times as well. Then, I started the solitary hansom ride home.

Later August 19, 1865 – It was good to see my family again, and the construction on the house is growing closer to completion; the masons have covered the first three floors with their work, and the interiors are all but finished except for the top floor where they await the masons before lining the wall.

August 20, 1865 – Again I dreamt of running, this time it was through the forest as I hunted after several deer. My feet were far more agile and quicker than my feet when I wake. Still I am haggard and cannot bear the morning light, hearing Abigail's sweet voice sing as Gloria brushes her hair and Gloria humming along makes me get out of the bed. They both noticed that I look rather worn, although I feel Gloria may have turned up an important clue as to what is causing my restless sleep. She noticed that my feet were muddy and I fear that I may have begun sleep walking. Tonight, I shall tie my ankle to the bed post and see if that does not help.

August 21, 1865 – I did not leave the room last night and do not recall any dreams, although I do not feel any better rested. Received response to my telegram, Thomas Owlcreek will be arriving the day before the next full moon.

Jack skimmed through more of the dates filled with more restless nights for Friedkin as he doted on his family and oversaw the construction of his house.

September 14, 1865 – I have returned from the village with the crucifix I commissioned from one of the artisans in town. It is the final adornment and the chapel will be complete. The idea had flowed from me as I told the artisan what I wanted and it changed as I spoke from my original concept to the Christ defiantly gritting his teeth as he controls the rage he feels at humanity. It was meant to be a great gesture of his love, but Abigail ran crying for her nanny when she laid eyes on it. Gloria also felt revulsion at it and refused to enter into the chapel if it were hanging on its walls. It is no matter; I will hang it above the altar and pray underneath it. How dare they blaspheme so against God and against me! I will see to it that when the minister travels through, we hold service here in the chapel under the watchful eyes of the crucifix.

September 15, 1865 – Was short with one of the cleaning ladies today, had the dream about chasing deer. This time, I caught one and feasted on it as if I was a beast of the woods. Would have liked to do that to the cleaning lady; the halls are still ripe with the pungent smell of something. Despite her claims of cleaning them repeatedly, I know she's lying.

I fear that I may have put my wife, dearest Gloria, into a brain fit. Today, while we were enjoying a glass of wine on the rear porch watching the woods before we were to dine, I smelled the most delicious aroma coming from the kitchen. She swore that she did not smell anything, but how such a savory flavor could pass by her, I knew not; she has always had a keen sense of smell. It fell upon me to investigate what the source of my mystery aroma was. I entered the kitchen and found it devoid of the help; they were no doubt preparing something in the cellar. Nonetheless, I found a pan that held some marinade with two cuts of beef that were to be our dinner. No doubt trying to flavor the beef. The smell was driving me mad, and I stuck my finger into it and licked it from the tip of my finger. It was a stronger taste than I expected, but it struck quite a chord with me. Finding a spoon lying nearby, I scooped a spoonful of the marinade and tasted it. This small portion did not satiate me, thus I went for a second spoonful when Gloria walked in. She shouted and fainted directly.

I had the stable boy fetch the local doctor and bring him back. He recommended that she be confined to bed for a few days. The doctor fears that she has suffered some sort of shock. I explained what had happened, and the doctor just made a confused face and saw himself out. Gloria confronted me about the marinade that I had found so delicious. The poor woman was under the impression that it is the blood from the raw beef and would not believe me otherwise. I must reprimand our cook; the beef was overcooked, and there was not even a hint of the marinade except in a few of the rarer cuts.

Gloria refuses to see me, which is a shame. Thomas comes tomorrow to put an end to the beast that was spotted in our woods last night. This beast is apparently getting bolder, it took one of our sheep from our rear pasture and butchered one of the rams. I would have liked for Gloria to have met Thomas, but I fear she may not be well enough.

September 16, 1865 – A bad omen is in the making. First, my dream, and then the horse the doctor left on last night was wandering near our stable this morning. Its leg had been cut, and I fear the bone broken. I took several of the servants and sought the doctor by the side of the road, fearing his injury. Now I think he will not be found. We came to a place in the road where the ground was saturated not from any rain - for there has not been any recently - but from blood. The beast of these woods has tasted human flesh, and the concern is that it may have sparked a desire for more within the beast's stomach. Thomas rode upon us as we made our way back to the house. After having brought his luggage in and eating a good meal, he has requested that I take him back to the bloodstained place so we may track the beast and set a trap for it. I will accompany him with my rifle. He is very excited for this new prey, although he feels it to be a mountain lion or some other indigenous large feline predator. We shall make our way soon and will most likely not return until tomorrow.

Jack noticed the scrawl of the next page and knew that something had happened; the neatly penned previous pages were replaced with a wild, quick hand that made it harder for Jack to read. Entries were not made every day anymore either.

September 18, 1865 – Dear God, a demon has taken residence in this forest. Thomas recreated the attack on the doctor and followed the tracks until they were lost among the rocks where I had found the paw print earlier. We set up in two separate hiding places some hundred feet apart. I must have fallen asleep during the night, for I awoke nude and lying on the ground some distance from my place. Shocked at my predicament, I went to find my friend. Thomas was not in his place either; his rifle had been fired, for I found the empty shell casings, but I found him near the rock formation. His body was ripped asunder while I slept, walking through the darkness unscathed. I found my clothes not far from my hiding place with my rifle, the butt was scratched, so my sleep-walking saved my life.

Great was my sorrow for my friend, and even greater was my shock when I realized that I had slept through the night into the early part of the afternoon. I did what I could to bury Thomas but did not finish before dark. I lay in the night with my rifle drawn tight around me and then awoke again, this time amongst a den of pine needles that had been matted down into some form of nest. Beside the place were the bloody clothes of the doctor and several bones of the missing livestock. Again, I had stripped during the night. What manner of curse has been placed upon me?

October 1, 1865 – I dream much more vividly now and fear that I am connected to the terror that roams here. I awake later and later in the afternoon often in the woods and have taken to hiding clothes in the stable for fear that someone within the house see me returning nude. Gloria is still confined to her bed; she grows weaker and weaker day by day. Abigail is my only solace. I always make sure to leave her with her nanny long before nightfall lest she get hurt and have taken to leaving my bed chamber windows open at night. I am no longer restless, merely frightened at the prospect of the setting sun and the terrors that come in the night.

October 13, 1865 – Abigail and her nanny have been killed. I saw it all and fear how I have seen such horrors. The nanny ripped to shreds guarding my daughter, such a heroic woman. Abigail snatched from her bed and taken as the beast leaped out the window with her and made its way through the fields into the woods where her flesh was made a feast. Damn my eyes and my body; why must I endure. I am the beast that prowls these lands. I awoke with the taste of blood on my tongue and the body of my perfect angel near. The servants we brought with us found me wandering in the woods naked and weeping. They assume I have succumbed to shock, for I have not been seen since she was taken two days ago. I fear that the monster inside me is leaking forward for longer periods. The beast broke through the front door and headed directly to the nursery. Gloria died upon the news of her child's death and my disappearance.

God rest her soul, the tragedy was too much for her already strained health. I have killed all that I love. The servants from the town have fled back to their village to avoid another night of the creature's rage. May Heaven or Hell have me, as I have come to the end of all. I am the destroyer of all that I have loved and all that was pure in this world to me and now I must be mine own destroyer.

November 3, 1865 – I will most likely never write in this journal again. After my last entry and realization of what must be done, I hung myself from the banister of the stairway on the top floor in hopes that none would find me. The demon inside will not let me die. I have since awoken this afternoon as a man, not in the horrid dreams of the monster. The servants are dead, destroyed and feasted upon in my bestial state, and I fear that the control this monster has on me will grow ever stronger and hold sway longer until one day I will never again appear and become all beast. As the sun loops around to let the shadows conquer, I feel the pull within me. I almost desire the change and carnage and weep at the *humanity lost. It appears I have only had a few hours of time as a man and must soon transform back into the destroyer. May God end my suffering soon before I cause more pain unto others.*

The journal ended with a few scratches of the quill upon the paper but no coherent words, and several of the rear pages were shredded. Jack flipped back through the journal; he began to see how the problem had started.

While Jack was reading through Friedkin's experiences, Owen was reliving the lives of the tobacco farmer who had moved into the area. It was with growing concern that he read as the terror currently facing Owen and Jack worked its malicious way into the lives of the previous tenants.

As Jack opened the volume in his hands, so did Owen. He skimmed the first dozen pages, reading how the man, James Smithson, had made his fortune in Virginia on a tobacco farm and wanted to attempt to make a second farm further inland to cut back on shipping expenses. He was able to purchase Friedkin's house, which had been abandoned, for a fraction of the value.

09/10/1908 – Arrived at the house today and found it with several areas that have become dilapidated since its abandonment. My first step will be to trim back the weeds that clog the path and refit the windows. Most of them are missing. According to local legend, some dog demon came and took the builder of this home and killed his wife and daughter. It appears to me that some animal has been in the building in the not too distant past. I will have the windows set with iron bars to prevent animals

from forcing their way in. I have a small crew of thirty that shall arrive
tomorrow and begin turning what I believe were pastures into fields that I
hope will spring ripe with tobacco.

Owen read the next few passages. They discussed the rebuilding
of the windows and fixing of some of the areas of disrepair, and the
beginning of their efforts to seed the ground. The only points of interest
were the arrival of James' young bride, Victoria, and a disappearance of
two of the workers. They left during the night to use the outhouse and
were never heard or seen afterward.

10/24/1908 – The men have gone into the village tonight to cavort
and drink. They shall come stumbling back at different times during the
day tomorrow, but they have worked hard and things are coming along.
The peculiar sounds that come from the forest still unnerve some of the
men, but since they have moved into the old servant's quarters we have not
had any more disappearances.

10/25/1908 – It is still early; I feel the sun may never rise. Last
night, Victoria was walking through the freshly plowed fields under the
night sky. I in my office looked out the window and saw the greatest
abomination I had ever thought possible. The dog demon the villagers
spoke of is real. I saw him as he defiled my wife. The terror and anger
swept over me. I awoke in my office a few hours later as the clock in the
hallway chimed the hour. I pray it was a dream; to confirm my suspicions
I went into her room and checked on Victoria. In the morning, I will
inquire of her, for she has scratches upon her shoulders and on her
forearm.

121
Friedkin's Curse

It is now ten and breakfast is past. I have done it over breakfast. I questioned my wife. She says that she does not remember getting the scratches, that perhaps she did it to herself in her sleep. I pray that it be true. My bride, the concubine of that foul demon I saw last night, I cannot entertain such thoughts lest I go mad. Perhaps I merely had dreams based on the old stories I have heard on the occasions I go into town.

10/26/1908 – Something made its way into the house last night. There were scratches on the floor near the dining hall. One of the cook's assistants was found mauled in the kitchen. Apparently, she stayed late in order to prepare for the next day. It was a gruesome sight. All signs point to the cellar as the point of entry. We have chained the iron door leading to the root cellar, as we have found it connected to a system of caverns. Victoria is acting strange. She seems cold and distant.

It approaches midnight, and God help us, something has torn through the chain. We heard it unto the upper floors; the sound came as a great rending. It was a heavy gauge chain and had been torn in half as if it were string. One of the workers is missing; we fear that our intruder may have taken him. Tomorrow, I must go into town and learn what I can of the lore of our monster. Victoria seems undisturbed by these occurrences.

10/27/1908 – I have discovered what I can. Now, I am on a quest. It seems that the legend tells these creatures have a weakness against silver. I have procured all that I could amongst the townspeople and have commissioned a blacksmith to make a chain of silver and a pendant of a wolf's head to hold it. This will bind the door and prevent further incursion.

Once more midnight comes and the devil runs wild. Our house is secure, but we could hear the beating upon the iron door and the growls *and howls of anger that filled the house until giving up, they fled. Perhaps we are safe after all. I have seen to it that Victoria sleeps with her silver crucifix about her neck. She is not content but has conceded to my wishes.*

Owen read through the next few entries. They told of the field workers leaving while the house servants would be staying behind and the occasional attempts by the beast to enter the house.

11/20/1908 – Victoria has told me that we are expecting child. I wish I could be overjoyed, but I fear it is the progeny of Satan and not my seed that is growing within her. We have not been intimate for some time. I must consult the doctor to determine this.

11/21/1908 – Sought out the doctor, but he refuses to come to our house. It seems that a doctor met his fate at the hands of the demon some years past and since then no doctor has been willing to traverse the lane. So it seems that I must bring Victoria to him.

11/22 1908 – The doctor found that she was almost two months with child, which does not bode well. The demon was with her only a month ago, but Victoria and I had not been intimate with one another since before he arrived, meaning either the devil has a child or another man has been with her. I shall truly question her tonight.

After dinner had passed, I questioned her, explaining the lapses in time. She swears her fidelity to me and undying love, claiming that the doctor must be mistaken, but is he not a learned man? I know that she did not lie to me. She lacks the nature to beguile and deceive, but the time still does not allow for it to be my child. I have sworn myself to her and as such, I must trust in her.

Owen read on; the entries were of business around the house while Victoria continued to show her pregnancy. Before Owen read the last entry, he noticed that the pages had marks on the ink and stains as if water had dripped on them.

12/18/1908 – I cannot describe the terror that awaited me in the earliest hours of this morning. I slumbered lightly as has been my way since coming here when Victoria called for me. There was fear in her voice, so I took my revolver from my bedside table and went to her in case the monster entered our home. Instead, I found her stomach engorged larger than it had been when she went to sleep. In pain and fear, she told me that something was wrong and begged that I help her. I could do nothing. Her stomach had swollen to capacity, and the skin burst. My wife died, and in her womb were four abominations of God. I picked up the bedside lamp, pouring the kerosene on my wife's body and the demon spawn that had killed her and ignited it with my own candle. The screams of the burning beasts was sweet music to my ears. It did not assuage my grief or make Victoria any less dear to me, for I knew that she would not have kept such terrors from me. God was merciful and kept her ignorant of the terrors she would have known. As those mewling cries died, long before the flames did, I heard the howling in the yard. I went to my office to write this and saw the evil that began the death sentence put upon my wife. It stares at me with such hatred knowing it was I that denied it the children it had wanted. I refuse to let it survive with my Victoria cremated in her own bed, her pure ashes mixed with those vile hell spawn. I have my pistol. If six shots should not be enough, then God let me pass quickly to the next world. Victoria, I love you.

Owen closed the journal, taking a deep breath. The fear he had was now compounded after having read of the beast's actions.

Owen lifted his eyes, fear shining brightly. "Jack, w-w-we've got p-p-problems." He stuttered.

Jack held up a finger and finished reading a page, then looked up at Owen. "We've got a lot of them, I'd say." Jack stared at Owen, noticing the sweat breaking out on his forehead and upper lip. "What did you find?"

"Our farmers were wiped out by something." Owen stopped and absently wiped his hand across his brow. "The way they describe it. It's almost. . . I think it's back."

Jack nodded. "Smart money says you're right. Let's just say that I've learned some interesting things myself. I think our enemy is on a hunting migration, following it over the course of years."

"Jack. It's not just hunting."

"What?" Jack took the book from Owen.

Owen showed the passages that had him so thoroughly upset. Jack stood up, the book falling forgotten from his hands onto the floor. He threw the mattress from the bed he and Emera had shared. Underneath it sitting atop the bed frame was the shotgun he had taken from a fallen soldier along with the ammunition. Urgently, he loaded the shotgun to capacity and laid the shotgun across his back in its sling. His .38 was tucked into the waistband of his jeans, Owen stood by the door waiting on him. They wasted no time explaining their actions to the soldiers staring at them but briskly walked down to the students' rooms. Ruby did not smile this time when they entered her room; the little girl could see the grim set of their faces and the shotgun protruding above Jack's shoulder.

Emera and Ameth were a bit unnerved by their expressions. Sliding the shotgun off of his shoulder, Jack handed the weapon to Owen. "We've got real problems. Stay in here with Owen. If you hear anything, just stay put. Owen, aim for the head." Jack exited and closed the door behind him.

Owen took a small chair from a nearby study desk, leaned it against the door, and sat in it. "What's going on?" Ameth asked, placing her hands on her hips.

"We've finished those journals Ms. Toews gave us. This whole thing doesn't look good."

Outside in the darkness, the beast waited. It had caught the scent and had learned patience, to strike only when the moment was exactly right. Or else it would fail, and that was not an option. The pale face of the moon began its rise across the sky.

Part 4: The Beast Among Us

Bridge sat behind the desk inhaling on his cigar, waiting. He knew the prey well enough. It would strike tonight. There were raised voices outside the door; Bridge instinctively placed his hand on the grip of his sidearm. The voices were silenced and something heavy landed on the floor. Sidearm in hand, aimed under the desk toward the door, Bridge waited. Jack barged into the room. Bridge moved his finger off of the trigger, but kept the hard set of his face. "What is the meaning of this?" He said, a low growl to his voice.

"I mean to save the lives of these people." Jack noticed that only one of Bridge's hands was on the desktop. "The werewolf is..."

"Did I not make it clear, civilian, you are not needed? From what I can tell from the private behind you, you've just assaulted one of my men. You will be confined to quarters." Bridge and Jack locked eyes, neither willing to blink first. The private gradually picked himself up off the floor and stepped up behind Jack.

"The door in the basement does not lead to an underground cellar. It's a series of caverns that lead out into the forest." Jack watched and was disappointed when Bridge did not make the connection. "Don't you see, if you don't guard the cellar door, he can come right in without us knowing it."

"Even if he could reason it out, how then would he find us and why would he try it?"

"For the same reasons you found on your previous hunts. I'm assuming that he's impregnated others." Bridge had a momentary lapse and surprise was visible on his face for a split second.

"Still, how would he know about the caverns?"

"Because, jackass, he built the house, the cellar, and did extensive research on the caverns. The werewolf is General Friedkin, the original owner of this house."

"And just why should I believe that?"

"Because I just read it in his journal. It was initially only a one-night event, but each time, the transformation would last longer; by this point he most likely never returns to the man he was." Bridge was beginning to believe Jack, so Jack pressed his argument. "One night after moving in, he became lost in the woods and drank rainwater out of a wolf's paw print."

"So?"

"According to Norse mythology, that was one of the methods by which one would become a werewolf." Jack took a deep breath, trying to calm himself. "Your werewolf is one of the great Union tacticians from the Civil War as well as the builder of this house. It also appears that he's come through here before."

"A migratory pattern?" Bridge asked.

"I think it's how he hunts. His path has led him back here again. If you check the areas where you chased him, I think you'll see patterns of unsolved murders and people vanishing in the past."

Bridge sat back in the chair, and with a wave of his hand, the private left the room. "What else can you tell me?"

"I don't know much, but I get the feeling you're aware of the breeding situation." Jack said. Bridge stiffened in his chair, the rage that had built in Jack was screaming inside of him to be set loose. "I see. Then, I guess you know full well what'll happen if it occurs."

Bridge nodded. "We've encountered a few situations."

"You should also know that I'm aware what Emera, Ameth, and these girls are to you: bait." Jack never broke eye contact from the old war horse at the desk.

Bridge chomped on his cigar. "It's getting late. You should join your friends."

Jack left the room past the dazed private. His anger at Bridge was immense. Jack had never felt such anger; it drew him inward causing him to ignore his surroundings. As he crossed the foyer to the stairs, a couple of soldiers passed him. Something struck him in the side of the head, sending him onto his side. He reached up to grab the side of his head where there was a white hot pain, but something grabbed his hand and rolled him onto his back. His vision was blurry and he saw an army green blur standing over him. With several rapid blinks, his vision cleared. The green blur was Jonas, a pistol in his hand. The black barrel aimed directly at Jack's head. Wilkes stood on the other side of Jack, giving furtive glances around to make sure that no witnesses were coming.

"Well, now, looks like third time's the charm." Jonas said smiling.

There was a staccato of gunfire from the hallway that Jack had emerged from; Jonas turned his head toward the noise. Jack pushed the gun away from his head, and sat up. Jonas squeezed the trigger as he turned to face Jack, the bullet lodged in the marble not far from Jack's head. With his left hand, Jack punched Jonas in the right knee then recoiled his elbow into his left, causing him to fall to his already hurt knees. With a quick twist, he pulled the pistol free of Jonas' hand and struck him full in the chin with the butt of the pistol. Jonas stayed in a kneeling position with his head resting on his chest, his shoulders slumped. Wilkes stood staring, not making a move. Jack stood and saw a dark-haired werewolf bolting from the hallway on all fours. It leaped, and Jack dropped behind the unconscious Jonas. The werewolf sailed over Jack and with a sickening crunch connected with Wilkes' ribcage. Wilkes squealed as the werewolf tore into his torso with a berserk rage. Blood spilled onto the floor, staining the marble, and pieces of flesh and muscle were thrown across the room. Jack, finding his feet, ran for the door. He was almost there when he heard the unmistakable sound of those blood-drenched claws tapping across the marble.

He opened the door and threw himself out of it, turning while in midair to face the door. He exhaled as he hit the sandbag barrier the soldiers had built. With a quick breath, he shouted: "Incoming!"

Soldiers began scrambling to the door with their weapons raised. Canva was giving hand signals to the approaching soldiers. Private Sands fumbled for the latch on his holster, and finally was able to retrieve his sidearm. He lay a few feet over from Jack. Jones spun into action and trained the heavy machine gun toward the door. He would not be able to get a shot unless it came outside. Holding his breath, he hoped it would. Jack couldn't see anything, but the werewolf should have emerged by now. Holding his breath, Jack rose into a crouch. The front sight on the pistol never left the open door. Cautiously, he lifted up while around him the soldiers closed in. He could see in the foyer. Jonas lay still slumped, just as Jack had left him while Wilkes lay dead in a pool of his own blood and viscera. Jack saw where deep grooves had been dug into the marble not far from the doorway. It looked as if the werewolf had dug its claws into the marble to stop itself. The beast had known the soldiers were outside.

Canva stood looking over Jack's shoulder. "Interior fire teams, report." Canva ordered into his communicator. He pressed a finger to his ear as he heard them sound off. "Full alert, we have a hostile in camp. Repeat, hostile in camp. Confirm lock down."

Jack started to go inside the door, but Canva placed a strong hand on his shoulder and kept him from entering. It looked like the bloody claw prints led away from the door, but Jack could tell the monster had not gone upstairs. Canva made a hand signal, and a small group of five soldiers stepped up to surround him. He firmly moved Jack out of his way and stepped into the door. "Follow the blood trail." Jack said.

Canva glanced over his shoulder at the man, and Jack pointed to the ground. Looking down, Canva saw the trail Jack meant. Weapons at the ready, the small contingent of troops made their way toward the hallway where the beast emerged, where the bloody tracks were leading them. Once they were to the mouth of the hallway, Jack ran across the foyer and up the stairs. At the top of the first flight of stairs, the fire team stopped him. Explaining himself, they called ahead to the other fire teams and let Jack proceed. He made it up to Ruby's room. Quietly, he opened the door and let himself in. The others looked at him anxiously. "We've got another one loose in here tonight." Jack said. He laid the sidearm he had commandeered from Jonas on the nightstand and pulled the .38 from his waistband. "They seem to have a good handle on it tonight, and it doesn't seem too interested in coming up here. After this, I get the feeling that Bridge will take this more seriously."

"So what do we do?" Emera asked fidgeting her hands nervously.

"We wait, and let the soldiers handle this one, unless it tries to get in here."

Canva led the small squad down the hallway. It wasn't wide enough for anything but a single line of soldiers. The men stayed a few

131

feet away from each other to allow for weapons clearance and also to prevent a domino scenario from occurring. They found the private that had been guarding General Bridge's door. He was ripped to pieces and strewn about the hall. The door to Bridge's makeshift office had deep gouges in it. Canva gave a tentative knock. "Sir." He called.

"Lieutenant," came the reply.

"Yes, sir."

"What's the sit rep?"

"Hostile has entered the compound. Has not tried to breach the higher floors. We're currently on the hunt."

"Good work, radio when you catch it. And remember, if it's our zero specimen, we want it alive."

"Yes, sir."

The bloody trail led away from the door and toward the far end of the hallway where bloody prints marred the door that lead outside. Canva edged along, halting the men just past the swinging kitchen door. He let his M-4 drop around behind him and withdrew his sidearm. Gently, he eased open the external door. Standing outside were several soldiers from the perimeter, their weapons trained on the door. They relaxed slightly at seeing Canva's face. He gave a quick nod and closed the door.

There was a shriek from behind him and the sound of the swinging door moving quickly. Turning, he saw the other men looking behind them as the white door swung in and out; meanwhile, one of the men had been pulled through the door and was now screaming furiously. Canva holstered the pistol and prepared his M-4. The soldier was thrown through the kitchen door, causing it to swing wide, and he crashed into the opposite wall, splattering it with his blood. In the light from the hallway, they saw the wolf, blood on its muzzle. It growled. The men opened fire, but the wolf quickly leaped behind a nearby counter, affording it cover. "Two of you pursue. The other two with me back to the foyer." Canva ordered as the two lead soldiers entered the kitchen to pursue the beast. Canva barked orders into his communicator. "I need three men in the foyer now, guarding the dining hall doors. All interior fire teams on standby; hostile is on the move."

They emerged from the hallway into the foyer and saw the three men that Canva had ordered kneeling in front of the dining room doors, their weapons at the ready and trained on the doors. They heard the sounds of gunfire, and then a large noise erupted from the hall. Canva looked down the hall in time to see the wolf burst through the hallway wall and rush through the exterior door that he'd already checked. The soldiers screamed and began firing. Canva ran at full speed down the hall, firing in three-round bursts. He hit the beast in the back and shoulders. It leaped to the safety of the forest and vanished in the shadows. There was a giant hole in the wall where the beast burst through the dining hall wall to escape the soldiers. Outside, the carnage was worse. One soldier had escaped unharmed. Two had sustained friendly fire incidents, one a fatal chest wound, the other merely a flesh wound. The other two were decimated; their quarry had come out the door right on top of these two and in seconds had destroyed them completely.

"I need a medic northwest perimeter." Canva ordered into the microphone and went inside as men from the neighboring squads arrived to guard the perimeter. Knocking on the office door, Canva opened the door and stepped inside. The door closed with a click. Canva stood at attention as Bridge faced the large window. "Sir, five dead and three wounded."

Canva could see Bridge's reflection in the window, and Bridge was looking at Canva. "Was it Zero?"

Friedkin's Curse

"I don't believe so, sir."

"Explain yourself." Bridge ordered, his face betraying no emotion.

"The color was wrong, sir."

"Very well." Bridge stood for a moment, looking once again out on the grounds of the school, the bright lights erasing the concealing shadows. "Lieutenant, it has come to my attention that what we believe to be a root cellar may in actuality be an underground cave system used to breach our defenses. I would like to place the M-249 and three support riflemen in the corridor down there. Also send some men down there to set up demolitions. If we're compromised, we'll bring it down, although it may serve as an escape if needs be."

Canva saluted. "Sir, yes, sir." He left, not waiting for the General to return the salute.

The breach would explain how the hostile had entered undetected. Canva saw the soldiers he had left in the foyer. He ordered two of them to the cellar to set up in the hallway. Once outside, he ordered Sands and another soldier to move the M-249 to the basement corridor, where they would remain until ordered elsewhere. Sands' shoulders relaxed at the order. "We believe it may be a breach point." Canva informed him.

The fear came back into the young man's face. Canva was glad, fear would keep him alert and it just might keep him alive.

In the excitement, Jonas had awoken and, seeing Wilkes, quickly deduced the situation and fled up the stairs before anyone started asking him questions. Jack sat on the floor. They had been listening to the gunfire downstairs, and then it had gone quiet. It seemed as though everything had calmed down. Emera let go of the breath she'd been holding since Jack had entered. Owen and Ameth did not seem overly concerned. Ruby seemed the most relieved. Emera sympathized with her younger sister, having been there with a monster prowling about outside. She could only imagine what the poor girl had felt. "You think it's safe to go back to the room?" Owen asked to no one in particular.

Ameth stood up and opened the door. "One way to find out." She said as she walked briskly down the hall.

Owen, still carrying the shotgun, followed her out of the room. "We'll see you in the morning. Try and get some sleep." Emera said as Jack put both pistols into his waistband, one on each side, a gunfighter without a holster.

Jack winked at Ruby, and she giggled. He was glad to see that the stress had not destroyed the sweet little girl he knew. Emera and Jack left the room together. "So, what's up with Ameth?" Jack asked.

Emera shrugged. "She's been a little antsy all night."

Jack made a noncommittal grunt as he saw the soldiers on the landing giving Owen trouble about the shotgun. With a gesture, Jack stopped Emera and stepped through the double doors.

". . . that doesn't belong to you." One of the soldiers was saying to Owen.

"Relinquish your weapon." The other one said as he began lowering his weapon from its current position, away from the ceiling and towards Owen.

Jack pulled the .38 and pointed it in the soldier's general direction. "This isn't one of yours." The soldier stopped, and his comrade reached for his M-4. Jonas' pistol was in Jack's other hand, bearing toward the other soldier. The tension with the soldiers and constant danger were beginning to fray Jack's nerves, though he tried to portray a calm demeanor. "This one, however is. Why don't you call your superior and

135
Friedkin's Curse

see if he minds us holding onto these for protection until you fellas have ended this situation? I mean, no point fighting amongst ourselves, especially with the wolves at the gate."

The soldiers exchanged glances, and then the first one called General Bridge. He explained the situation, and waited for his orders. "Yes, sir." He said as he turned back toward Jack and Owen. "You gentlemen can keep the weapons."

Jack placed the pistols back into his waistband. "Thanks." His nerves began to relax as some of the tension that had built in his stomach eased.

Owen took the shotgun and went up the stairs. Jack opened the door, and held it as Emera came walking out. She tried not to look at the soldiers, the flush in their cheeks showimg their embarrassment. Once they were out of ear shot of the troops, Emera finally spoke. "What are you trying to do?"

"What do you mean?"

"You know what I mean. They wanted that gun Owen had and you decide to pick a fight with them. Do you want to get shot? Because if what you said is true, these guys are killing their own."

"Emera ..."

"I don't care, Jack. I don't care why you did it; if you want to get killed, you do it some other time. With everything else going on, I do not need to lose you." Her voice broke, and Jack noticed the tears trailing down her cheeks.

He put an arm around her shoulders. He wasn't the only one noticing the tension; Emera's shoulders were knotted with it. "I'm sorry, babe. I didn't think. I'll be more careful." He lifted her chin up so he could look her in the eyes. "I promise." Some of the tension went out of her shoulders, and she hugged Jack. He kissed her forehead. "Let's get back to the room."

Emera wiped the tears away as they went up the rest of the stairs to the top floor where they would be staying another night. Two more than they had planned on, and God only knew how many more they'd be there. Bridge surmised that it would not take him more than another day or two to finally have his opponent. The beast they knew as Hostile Zero had other plans.

Laid out before the beast was the town of Mead's Hall, and deep in the savage mind of the beast a flicker of his previous tactical mind flared, and the beast devised a plan.

It was almost two in the morning when Ameth got up to leave the room. "What's going on?" Owen asked, causing Jack to wake up.

"Just got to go to the little girl's room." Ameth said and left.

Owen and Jack drifted right back to sleep. The tension of the last few days and adrenaline that had coursed through them so much recently left them spent and needing their rest. Something shook Jack's shoulder. With a start, Jack reached for the pistol wedged between the mattress and box springs, but it was only Owen. "Ameth hasn't come back yet?" Owen said, still semi-asleep.

Jack yawned. "How long?"

"Close to half an hour." Owen said. Even in his half-asleep state, Owen's concern for his wife showed through.

Jack sat up and woke Emera. "Sweetie, Ameth's been in the bathroom for a while so we're going to go check on her."

Emera looked at them through the hazy shades of waking and nodded her understanding. She rolled over and pulled the blankets back up to her neck. Jack had the pistols in his waistband, and Owen carried the shotgun. Everything seemed quiet in the hallway. Nothing seemed out of place, which only served to enhance their apprehension. The guards placed on the landing had been reassigned earlier in the evening, so it was just Owen and Jack. The door to the chapel stood slightly askew. Owen was headed through the second set of doors, while Jack held back. There was a smudge of something on the door frame, and he wanted a closer look at it. "Jack?" Owen was standing with the door open, looking over his shoulder at his friend.

Jack motioned him onward. "Just want to check on Wierzbowski."

Owen let the door close and continued creeping down the hall. The doors were closed, and the bathroom was at the far end of the hall. Nothing stirred as he made his way down the hallway. Jack stood at the door frame looking at the crimson stains. It looked like blood. Retrieving the M-9 he had taken from Jonas, he pulled back the slide, chambering a round. He held his breath without thinking about it. Pushing the door open, he led with the pistol, sweeping from side to side. He didn't see anything resembling a target. The feral Christ hung on the cross overseeing the carnage in the room. Blood coated the floors. The bottom half of the crucifix was covered in blood. Wires sparked from the communication's equipment that had been set up. Jack saw Wierzbowski's body lying behind the equipment. He had been stabbed numerous times and his own knife was sticking out of his throat. Jack checked the chapel for any signs of the attacker and ran out the door, checking the landing to make sure there was no immediate threat. Then, he sprinted down the previous hallway and checked on Emera. She was still sound asleep.

Closing the door, he sprinted after Owen. As he opened the door, he saw that Owen was almost to the end of the hall. "Hurry!" Jack called after him.

A few doors opened and soldiers stuck their heads out, still somewhat asleep but ready to take up arms as needs be. Owen looked back over his shoulder and saw Jack running down the hallway toward him. "We've got issue. Sound the alarm." Jack said to the nearest soldier.

The soldier turned and ran down the hall, most likely to the next landing where the guards had been placed. Owen ran the rest of the way to the bathroom, ignoring caution, just needing to make sure Ameth was safe. Gunfire broke out on the floor beneath them, and Jack halted in his steps and listened. It was the staccato fire of the M-4, intermittently with the boom of a shotgun. Owen never slowed his pace. The soldiers began to file out, shirts unbuttoned, rifles in hand. Jack began to pick up his speed to catch up with Owen. Reaching the bathroom, Owen slammed his shoulder into the push door, and it opened. Ameth stood straight up. Water was dripping down her face as water ran from the tap in the sink. "Are you okay?" Owen asked.

"I just don't feel too good." Ameth looked at Owen, and then saw Jack reach the door. "Why?"

"Something's in the building." Owen said.

"Oh," Ameth responded. "Give me a minute?"

Owen nodded and closed the door. "So, it's on three?" Owen asked.

"Something is." Jack chewed on the corner of his lip, something he only did when he was running through facts trying to make a decision. "I don't think it's the only thing in here." Owen tilted his head slightly, giving Jack a puzzled look. "The chapel's been destroyed and

Friedkin's Curse

Wierzbowski with it. I don't think it did that and then went downstairs and entered the hall without disturbing the guards at the door. Plus it killed Wierzbowski with his own knife."

"So we have a monster and a possible murderer in here?"

Jack shrugged and adjusted his grip on the pistol. Ameth exited the restroom, and they began walking down the hall back to the room. Jack and Owen flanked Ameth. The trio came to the landing, and Ameth stopped. Owen noticed and stopped, too. Jack stopped when his was the only footstep he heard. Both of the men turned toward Ameth. She drew in a deep breath. "Isn't it wonderful?" She asked.

Both men took a whiff of the air but didn't smell anything different. "What?" Asked Jack.

She pulled the pistol from Jack's hand and threw it behind her. "Hey," Owen said, coming closer.

There was a deafening crack as Ameth backhanded Owen. His body went limp, hit the stairs and rolled down them. He came to rest on the third floor landing. The soldiers were too busy dealing with the threat on that floor to notice him. The shotgun had landed near the stairs but had not gone over them; the only problem was that Ameth stood closer to it than Jack. "As I was saying, isn't it wonderful, the smell of fresh blood?" She smiled revealing, a row of sharp canine teeth as her eyes turned a luminous shade of amber.

"Shit," Jack said as he pulled the revolver from his waistband.

He looked down the barrel at Ameth's contorting face but could not bring himself to shoot. Her hands with elongated fingers ending in the obsidian claws slashed at him. With a backward roll toward the hallway where Emera was sleeping, he sat up and fired. The bullet went cleanly through Ameth's knee. The thing that used to be Ameth fell to the floor, and began a scream that turned into a howl halfway through. Lean muscle rippled and changed the contour of her frame as joints shifted and extended, hair appearing where before had been porcelain white skin. The knee was still not able to support the weight of the beast, but Jack could see it mending. He fired another shot into the other knee. The werewolf, which no longer bore any semblance to Ameth, slashed at him in futility. It began to pull itself toward him, using its fore claws to drag the menacing, powerful, vicious frame toward him. He pushed open the door and stood up. Emera was standing in the doorway, looking toward the door. "Get inside. Barricade the door." He ordered.

"Get in here."

Jack came to the door and stepped inside. He took a close look around. "Get on the other side of the bed."

Emera stepped onto the mattress and crossed over the bed. She went to her knees using the bed as cover. Using the door frame to steady himself, Jack kneeled and took aim on the double doors. Patience was the only advantage he had. The animal on the other side of the door would charge as soon as it could stand, if not sooner. He took three deep breaths to slow his heart. Not because of what he had just witnessed or fought, but because when it was over, he'd have to tell Emera that her sister was lost to them, and Owen may be dead.

Straining his ears, Jack could hear the shuffling movements from the other side of the door. He stayed in his place with the pistol aimed long enough for fatigue to set in, and his gun hand began to quiver lightly. There was no sound of imminent danger coming from the landing, so Jack lowered his hand, letting the muscles rest. The gunfire from the third floor had died out, and silence hung thick in the air. No sound came from the landing. Other than Emera and his own breathing, Jack could not hear

141
Friedkin's Curse

anything. He stood up and stepped out into the hallway, his grip on the pistol tightening. "Jack!" Emera screamed.

The sound of glass breaking told Jack everything he needed to know. Reaching in the door, he saw the dark shape rising in front of the shattered window, bars pushed inward and ripped from the brick. He grabbed Emera by the arm and pulled her over the bed and out the door, closing it behind him. "Run!" He ordered as he began to backpedal away from the door.

The Ameth wolf had went out through the roof doorway on the other hall and come over the building to get them. To Jack's surprise the iron bars had given way. The door shook in its frame and a large crack appeared in the center of the heavy wooden door. Another thud, and the wood splintered more. With the third impact, the door was split almost completely in half. Jack could see the body of the werewolf through the splintered wood. He wasn't sure how much good a shot would do through the door, so he waited. All of his spare ammunition to the .38 was inside the room with the werewolf.

Finally, the top half of the door flew into the hallway, and staring over the jagged bottom half was the Ameth wolf. Saliva fell in rivulets as the werewolf's craving for human flesh became greater. Putting one foot on the bottom half of the door the wolf began to leap over it. With one well-placed shot through that exposed leg, Jack was able to knock the werewolf off balance and landing on the jagged edges of the door. A howl of pain and anger rose out of the beastly throat, and the werewolf began to pull itself up off the jagged splinters. Turning, Jack ran for the landing. Emera stood near the top of the stairs, looking at Jack. In her arms was the shotgun, picked up from where it had fallen from Owen's hands. Jack had forgotten about it.

Running over to Emera, he took the shotgun from her. "Go downstairs, get the soldiers."

She ran down the stairs. Jack turned back to the doors; he could hear the werewolf coming. A slight limp from the bullet, and the muscle damage sustained from the door was healing but was still preventing the werewolf from rushing Jack at full-force. He heard Emera's strangled cry and realized that she had found Owen. The double doors were ripped from their hinges, and the werewolf stood there, shreds of the shirt Ameth had been wearing still clinging to it. Jack raised the shotgun and stared into the slightly luminescent eyes of the beast. Despite the horror consuming him, and the desire to kill this monster, he could not. He knew the person inside and that made it all the harder to do. Ameth charged at him, still with a limp. Jack raised and fired. His shot had strayed from what he had wanted to do but still stopped the werewolf, hitting her in the right hip; Jack had wanted a gut shot. The force of the impact spun the werewolf around and laid it out on the ground.

The hip where the leg had connected had been torn away; the leg was still attached by some of the joint and a few small strands of muscle and tendon. The werewolf raised itself into a sitting position and began pulling itself back to rest against the wall. Jack stood watching in amazement as the decimated joint began to grow bone; tendon and muscle began to slither, reconnecting and growing back. Putting the shotgun to his shoulder, Jack waited to fire. He aimed for the head but could not pull the trigger. The creature looked at him and began to growl fiercely. The werewolf's head was suddenly laid open by a three-round burst from an M-4. Jack stood, unable to move for a moment before turning to see Canva kneeling, his M-4 still in position and smoke rising from the barrel. While he had been contemplating what to do, a small group of soldiers had come upstairs behind him. Standing on the landing with the smell of gunfire hanging in the air, Jack watched the soldiers. Canva stood and stared at Jack, while two of the accompanying soldiers went and inspected the body. As Jack and Canva stood facing each other, there was a gargled noise from behind Jack. Spinning around, he saw a soldier lying over the legs of the werewolf his throat ripped out, as another had his stomach ripped open, intestines spilling out, all the while the soldier tried to bring his shotgun around. His screams of pain were the worst sound that Jack had heard. Raising the shotgun, Jack closed his eyes. "God forgive me." He whispered and pulled the trigger.

The screaming continued, and when Jack opened his eyes, there were tears blurring his vision. The soldier was now laying on his back, screaming in sheer agony. The werewolf's neck and lower jaw had been hit by the slug, causing it to explode, and the spinal cord had been severed. A few tendons were the only thing holding the head on. The vertebrae glistened in the light. The werewolf's form began to change becoming for the last time the oldest sister of Ruby and Emera. The shotgun was heavy in Jack's hands as he went down the stairs, ignoring the soldiers coming up. At the third floor landing, he saw Owen on a stretcher. A medic was attending to him as Emera stood over him in tears. She saw Jack and her tears came more quickly. "Ameth?" She asked through the sobs, which threatened to escape if she said anymore.

Jack could feel the lump in his throat and the tears rolling down his cheeks. He merely shook his head. Emera fell to her knees and sobbed as a grief-filled wail tore from her throat. Jack knelt in front of her and held her. She cried into his shoulder for the next half an hour, both of them kneeling on the third floor landing. Owen had been wheeled away by some soldiers; he was alive. After the initial shock of losing her sister wore off, Emera stood up, not bothering to wipe the tears from her face. "I've got to tell Ruby." She said between sobs.

Jack stood with her and went to inform the youngest sister of the tragedy that had struck their family. Ruby was in her room, the door askew on the hinges. Emera went into her younger sister, who was already crying. Jack fixed the door in place as best he could and stayed outside to let the sisters have their time to grieve alone. He went looking for Owen. At the bottom of the stairs in the foyer, he found him, a medic beside him as some of the soldiers argued about treating him. "Why does he get treatment? He ain't one of us." Demanded a soldier with a scar running down the side of his face.

"I say we put one in his head. It'd be a mercy." Said Jonas standing behind the others.

Jack pumped a round into the chamber of the shotgun. The noise caught everyone's attention; they stared at the man on the steps, a shotgun poised in his hands pointing toward the congregated soldiers. The men were afraid to meet his eyes. They knew the look in them; it was the look of a man very near the breaking point; a man with little to lose. Walking the rest of the way down the stairs, Jack never moved the shotgun off of the soldiers. Even when the soldiers began to walk away, Bridge came up behind Jack. A solid pat on the shoulder told Jack how close the man was. "Good job," Bridge said.

Jack lowered the shotgun and faced the General. "What's going to happen to Owen?"

Bridge grinned like a wolf in a sheep pen. "We'll do everything we can for him, but we're limited here."

"What about the chopper?"

"Radio equipment's torn to hell, I've got some boys looking at it right now; if we get it running, I promise we'll get your friend out of here. Despite the carnage, I feel this may have been very productive."

"How?" Jack asked.

"Well, we've found his intended target don't you, think?"

"No."

Bridge licked his upper lip. "Well, son, it seems fairly obvious that there aren't any more choices." Jack stood in silence, listening to the General. "We think we can catch it with the proper bait."

"No." Jack said in a voice barely above a whisper.

"What did you just say?" Bridge asked, leaning closer to Jack, daring him to repeat himself.

"No," came the response.

Bridge slammed his fist down on the stair railing. "What in the hell do you mean 'no'? Perhaps you didn't notice, but it's my ball game. You'll do what you're told. Now, the girl is going to stay with us in a secure room. You can either like it or..."

Bridge never got a chance to finish; Jack weighed his options. Hitting the man would only take him out of the fight. He needed to do something to become a part of it. Jack stopped on the last stair. "Get the radio fixed and get that chopper in here." Jack walked up the stairs, and Owen lay on a stretcher and dreamed the dreams of a man whose mind was buried under morphine.

Canva stood beside the General. "Sir, what do you want me to do about him?" Canva asked.

"Do? Nothing. That boy will be too much trouble if we try to stop him, and the girl will be trouble if we kill him. Let him think on his options. In the meantime, have the men bring in the field radio equipment from my Humvee."

"Yes, sir." Canva said as he ran out the front door.

The dawn was almost upon them. Bridge knew his nemesis would not give up without getting the girl, and that would be his downfall. He mused to himself as he turned to go back to his office, but Canva stopped him. The lieutenant burst back through the front door and ran toward Bridge with the field headset extended in his massive hand. "General, we have problems."

Bridge listened for a few seconds. It seemed there had been some trouble in the town last night. No confirmations, but no one was responding to anything. Bridge put the headset back on the body of the field radio and looked at Canva oddly. "Lieutenant, would you care to explain why I should care? We've seen Hostile Zero tear up towns before."

"Yes, sir, but I don't think this is a frustrated slaughter. A National Guard patrol was sent after massive calls about rioting flooded local 9-1-1 centers. They can't find anything."

"Weekend soldiers, doesn't surprise me."

"Sir, with all due respect, they found blood and shell casings from small arms fire and even the firearms, but they can't find any bodies. They've found a few limbs and that's it."

"Canva, what are you suggesting?"

"What if it's raising an army of its own?" It was a simple question, but one that struck the General to the core.

"Get the local air base on the horn; I want F-16s pumped and primed, armed with napalm. Tell them to also arm their Apache 'copters with incendiary and frag rounds. If your theory is right, we may have to burn the entire forest tonight. I also want minute-by-minute satellite updates, any movements or heat signatures. Have any satellites rerouted so we do not have blackouts, code Alpha Beta Tango."

Bridge felt the slight quicken to his pulse as he walked back to the office while Canva went to set up the radio in the dining room and complete Bridge's orders. It was anticipation with a tinge of fear. They had fought a few packs of these monsters. Never more than eight or ten, but now his men would be going up against a fighting force of possibly several hundred. He had no delusions; there was a chance that he might survive this with some of the men, but it was a razor-thin chance. His chances of taking the target alive had disappeared entirely, but that didn't mean he had to let the bastard live. Ordering the private at his door inside, Bridge gave him explicit instructions. He was to procure an M-4 and a shotgun with a bandolier of ammo for each, and two fragmentation grenades. As the private left, to go speak with the sergeant major about procuring the weaponry, Bridge examined the bars on the window. They were solid and sturdy, set deep into the mortar of the house. His only vulnerable point would be the door. If he became trapped in here, the fragmentation grenades would ensure that he could at least take any of them in the room with him.

Bridge spoke into the microphone on his collar. "Attention, men, it looks as if we may be facing superior numbers tonight, but that doesn't mean shit. We have the superior technology, weaponry, and training. We are the United States Army and we will stand our ground and win our battle. This is General Bridge, over and out." He sat down in the leather chair and felt its cushion. The trap was the key to victory. He would have to put the girl someplace defensible.

While Bridge sat and ran through the different scenarios of the coming battle, Jack went to visit Emera. She was still in Ruby's room. It was oddly empty; that was when Jack noticed the empty top bunk and even more disturbing was the way the mattress had been ripped apart. Jack had never found out what caused the gunfire from this floor. "What happened?"

Ruby looked up her eyes red and puffy from crying. Ruby pointed her finger up toward the top bunk. "She became one." A few fresh tears rolled down her cheeks and then no more.

Jack assumed it was all she could muster, but that explained what had happened. Emera tucked Ruby into her bunk to get some rest, since she had not been able to get any previously. Emera did not look much better than Ruby.

Every time a thought of Owen or Ameth began to rise in Jack's mind, he pushed it down deep. He was upset over what had happened, but he could not let it overpower him. Not yet. Emera looked at Jack. "What's wrong?" She asked, putting her hand in his.

"Do you remember what we told you about the tobacco farmer's journal? About his wife?" She nodded. "Apparently, this thing is on the prowl for more. From what I've gathered, it happens most places where they've chased it. And now they think that you're the..." Jack couldn't finish the sentence.

Emera's hand clenched Jack's. "Why?"

"There aren't any other candidates." Jack could see the fear and anguish creeping up her face. "They want to use you as bait tonight."

"Okay." She said.

"No," Jack could not believe what he had heard. "You can't trust them; they still aren't telling us everything. And after everything I've seen so far, I don't think they have any idea what the hell they're doing."

"Jack," Emera said his name in the familiar, low, hushed voice of a lover. "I'll only do it if you're there to help them watch over me. I can't stand by another night and watch more people die, especially if it's because this thing is after me."

The firm set of her eyes and jaw told Jack that the argument was over. She would not change her mind now. "Okay, I'll go talk to them."

"I'll go with you. I need something to eat." Jack noticed that his stomach had also started making small, gurgling sounds; with the adrenaline pumping through his system, his hunger had never even occurred to him.

Once on the first floor, Jack headed for the office where Bridge sat running through his scenarios while Emera headed toward the dining room doors. Near the back of the foyer by the phone bank was Jonas. His jaw still hurt, but he'd pay Jack back. Then, he laid his eyes on Emera; licking his lips, he took a deep breath. He thought he could smell the slightly sweet scent of shampoo and lotion. They were headed in different directions. Jonas knew this was his chance to get what he wanted and hurt Jack at the same time. Once Jack went down the hall, he started following Emera as she went into the dining hall. Jonas had just left there a few minutes earlier and knew that no one else was in there.

He slid in the door before it had closed and watched as Emera walked between the tables; she still had not noticed the lecherous man following her. Jonas just stood watching her; he liked the way she moved. Silently, he followed, gradually closing the gap between them until she was in the kitchen and Jonas came stepping through the door. Ahead of Emera was the preparation table where most of the sandwiches had been made from the day before. It was stainless steel and freshly cleaned. Sitting off to the side was a portion of the silver dining set, the serving fork, ladle and several other utensils. Jonas grabbed her by the back of the head and pushed her against the preparation table. He forced her head down and bent her over the table. She started to scream, but with the weight of Jonas pinning her to the table, she could hardly breathe. "Now, bitch, I'm going to do what I've been wanting to do since I saw your sweet ass. And your boyfriend can't do shit about it."

Emera could feel the bulge growing in Jonas' pants; panic exploded in her mind, and she began reaching for anything of use. Her hand gripped the handle of something and she blindly stabbed behind her. Suddenly the pressure was off, and a scream erupted from behind her. She didn't look. Climbing over the table, Emera ran through the swinging doorway and emerged in the hallway. "Jack!" She screamed.

The office door flew open, and Jack stood in the hallway shotgun pointed toward the floor. Emera covered the ground as fast as she could and almost toppled Jack as she hugged him. "He was going to..." Emera squeezed Jack even harder and then the kitchen door she had just left swung open.

"Christ!" She heard Jack exclaim.

She felt the hand on her shoulder. It was Jack and he moved her around behind him. Emera saw the thing standing outside the kitchen doorway. It was the soldier, Jonas, his face was gaunt and pale, with long strands of hair dangling from his face. One side of his mouth had begun to wrap around onto the side of his head, showing sharp teeth, and his eyes were larger and amber-colored. Sticking out of his side was the silver serving fork, the sound of sizzling flesh and smoke rising from the wound. His one hand was outstretched toward Emera. "Holy Mary, Mother of God." Said Bridge, standing in the doorway looking at the thing stumbling down the hallway.

Friedkin's Curse

Jack raised the shotgun. Jonas looked at him, and even with the change in his eyes, the one thing that had not changed was the sheer hatred for Jack. "Fuc..." was all that dribbled out from the elongated mouth on Jonas' face before Jack obliterated it with the shotgun.

The body did a complete somersault and landed on the floor in an unmoving heap. Several soldiers came in through the door with their weapons ready. They saw Jack, smoking shotgun in hand, and Jonas slowly returning to normal. "Get that out of here and burn it." Bridge ordered. He held out his hand and led Emera into the office. Jack followed them. Bridge poured her a small glass of whiskey. "It'll help your nerves."

She took the shot and grimaced. "What happened?" Jack asked, rubbing the back of her neck.

"I went into the kitchen to get something to eat, and then he pushed me onto a table. He was saying the..." She stopped and shook her head, trying to forget the attempted violation.

"We don't have to talk about that part." Jack said, looking at Bridge; the man did not offer any disagreement. Not that Jack would have cared if he did. "What did you do to him?"

"I grabbed something and jabbed it backwards. He let go and screamed. That's when I ran into the hall and called you."

Jack kissed the top of her head. "Good job, honey. You must have hit him with that fork."

"That doesn't explain why he turned into that." Bridge said.

"The fork was silver. He could have been injured last night. I mean, he was unconscious when we were initially attacked, so if he'd have been wounded, he might've never known or knowing how the wounded get treated, he kept his mouth shut." Jack thought for a moment. "The lack of the moon probably prevented him from turning completely."

"We've tried silver on Hostile Zero, and it never slowed him down."

"Maybe over time, the reaction loses its potency." Jack's eyes darted across the desk, and then he looked up. "It's only a reaction that younger ones have. The first one we encountered after you arrived; she was burned by a silver pendant, and just now. It's the only explanation. Over time, it becomes less effective."

"So, how does this help us?" Bridge asked.

"Do you guys have any claymore mines?"

Understanding flashed in Bridge's eyes. "I'll get the men on it. By the way, it looks like we can get your friend carried out of here before nightfall."

"Thanks," Jack said. "So, think about what I suggested for tonight."

Bridge nodded. Jack took Emera and held her close to his side as they went upstairs. They did not go back to their room but instead went to Ruby's. She was sitting up wide-eyed as the door opened. "Hey, Rube, thought maybe we could crash here."

Ruby's shoulders relaxed when she realized who had come in. She just nodded and lay back down with her back toward them, facing the wall. Emera sat down on the small twin mattress. "Jack, that man."

"Shhh," he squeezed her hand. "He won't give us any more trouble. And don't confuse him with a man; he was a monster worse than the ones in the forest."

Emera nodded her head, and her eyes seemed to soften as she processed what had happened, but she had stopped it. Jack had ended the threat permanently, but she had saved herself. It was this knowledge that let her lay down beside her sister and sleep. Jack pulled the blanket off of the ripped-up top bunk and laid on the floor, using a nearby stuffed animal for a pillow.

Jack wasn't sure how long he had been asleep, when a soft knock at the door came through. He opened the door and saw a soldier there at attention. "The General wanted me to inform you that your friend was being evacuated in ten minutes."

His message delivered, the soldier left. Jack woke Emera and told her what was happening. She insisted on going to see him off. Emera woke Ruby and told her about Owen; Ruby decided she wanted to see him off as well. The trio was in the foyer when the medic, a Dr. Lindstrom, came into the room as two soldiers wheeled the gurney with Owen on it to the door. An IV had been put into his arm and a saline bag was hanging above his head. Then, they heard the sounds of the helicopter coming into land. Owen was drifting in and out of his morphine-laced dreams. Emera and Ruby each gave him a kiss on the cheek. Jack stood by as two of the airmen with the helicopter came in and carried the gurney out the door. Dr. Lindstrom went with them. There were two other medics with the deployed soldiers, and Owen might need medical attention on the flight. Dr. Lindstrom had volunteered to go with him. Jack, Emera, and Ruby stood in the open doorway, watching as Owen was carried into the back of the helicopter, its ramp raised, and it lifted off.

All three of them hoped Owen would be safe, because Jack and Emera knew what was expected to happen tonight while Ruby had a feeling of dread at the thought of the setting sun. Ruby and Emera returned to Ruby's room to get some more sleep so they could be prepared for the long night ahead. Jack made a detour to their room first. He took all the ammunition for the shotgun and .38 that he had procured. He was sure he could get more if he needed it. His errand done, he returned to the Ruby's room and found her and Emera asleep on the small twin bed.

The helicopter was off the ground and moving above the trees toward the nearest Air Force base with medical facilities, but only Dr. Lindstrom knew that Owen would not live that long. He had been given specific orders from General Bridge. "Go with him, but make sure he doesn't make it to that base alive." Bridge had said, standing in the office he had commandeered.

Dr. Lindstrom was a soldier first and a doctor second, so he had no problem obeying orders even if it violated the Hippocratic Oath he had taken upon becoming a doctor. He looked at the airmen in the cockpit of the helicopter and the one who was sitting in the back with him. Had the man been awake, he might have seen what happened, but he was resting his head against the hull sleeping. He would have seen Lindstrom retrieve the hypodermic needle from his little doctor's bag. The syringe was full of morphine, more than enough to force an overdose. Inserting it into the IV line, Lindstrom depressed the plunger, sending the contents of the syringe into Owen's veins, but the man was asleep and saw nothing. Lindstrom kept monitoring Owen. After a few minutes, his pulse began to weaken. Lindstrom waited a minute before telling the pilot that the man was fading. They raced toward the base as Owen's heart beat slower and slower. They were coming in to land when his heart stopped beating. The medical teams at the base were unable to revive him, despite their best efforts.

While Owen forfeited his life, Bridge sat behind his desk, no remorse for killing an innocent man. He told himself it had to be done; once Owen was in the hands of the Air Force, it would be impossible for Bridge to contain him, and risk of the operation leaking to the public increased greatly. Orders were to keep the mission classified at all costs, to prevent public panic or some such. Bridge did not care about the why, only that his mission was accomplished fully. His men were wrapping the silverware around the claymore mines they had. These were going to be set as a tripwire, so that any frontal assault would be met with hot, silver shrapnel. Bridge had to admit that Jack had come in handy on more than one occasion. This did not endear Jack to the General, though. Bridge had seen many men under his command die and had long since stopped thinking of people as anything other than expendable.

The sun was hanging low in the sky, when the soldiers came around gathering the remaining students, Jack and Emera among them. They were being escorted down to the auditorium; there were only two entrances to the room, so it was the easiest to defend. Jack noticed soldiers at the far end of the hall with wire and tin cans. On the landing, he discovered what they were for, he could see the wire strung across the stairs at two different locations, and each end of the string was attached to the pin of a grenade. The grenades were sitting in the tin cans and the tin cans were attached to rail posts on the stairs. Anything coming from upstairs would get a surprise and notify the men in advance of any infiltration.

Sands and three other men were assigned to the cellar corridor to ensure they were not breached through the underground caverns. Jones was smiling in his perch behind his .50 caliber. He knew what the night held, and he was more than happy to meet it. Royston was in the front seat, his M-4 positioned to fire out the driver's side window. His main purpose for being stationed there was to hand Jones more ammunition. The large trucks they had arrived in had been brought to their side to create a funnel into what the soldiers were thinking of as the kill zone. The main contingent of men was stationed near the front doors. Large ropes of C-4 had been posted at the tops and bottoms of the columns. In the event that things went badly, they could be detonated and the small roof section would collapse to barricade the main entrance. The doorway at the end of the hallway where Bridge had taken his office was barricaded with several large bookshelves from the study and was nailed shut to keep it from being breached.

All of the snipers, had been repositioned to the corner rooms on the third floor where they could concentrate their fire easily into any direction that was needed. The corner rooms had two windows as opposed to one, these windows faced into the forest on the side of the school or the front or rear of the school, depending on which side the room was on. Only one man was placed on the roof this man's purpose was to direct the soldiers as needed and keep an eye on the battle. Lt. Canva and a contingent of twenty men were guarding the auditorium. General Bridge was making his station in the office. From there, with the radio, he could call in any air support as needed.

Bridge's ear piece came alive as the moon rose into the sky while its daytime counterpart fell beyond view. "General," came the signal from Sergeant Wiine, the man monitoring the repaired radio equipment in the chapel.

Friedkin's Curse

Depressing the lever on the side of the microphone, Bridge responded. "Report."

"Sir, we have a massive mobilization on our front, over."

"Distance?"

"Three to three and a half miles, just entering the northern quadrant of grid six, over."

"Roger that. Sergeant, I need you to keep me informed of all movement, over and out." Bridge took the handle for the field radio in his hand and prepared the order; he looked over the map and found the coordinates he needed. "Little Red, this is Big Bad Wolf, copy?"

"Roger, Big Bad Wolf, this is Little Red, over." Came the response.

"Little Red, we need a wall of fire at grid six, two and three kliks south of grid five, over."

"Sir," responded the base representative. "If we hit that with napalm, the entire region could blaze for weeks."

"Son, I don't care. If you don't do as ordered there are a lot of soldiers going to die. Do you understand, over?"

"Yes, sir. This is Little Red. Fire wall is inbound E-T-A: three minutes, sir, over."

"Big Bad Wolf, over and out." Bridge laid the handset on the table and waited; in three minutes the night was going to light up, and if he was right, most of his troubles would be handled as well.

Sergeant Wiine came back over the earpiece. "Sir, eye in the sky is reporting that hostile forces are vanishing, over."

Bridge sat up attentively. The satellite imaging could be wrong, but if the hostiles were taking to underground, they would be disappearing from view. Underground, they would also be able to avoid the napalm.

"Roger that, sergeant," Bridge opened the squad channel and spoke directly to his men. "Men, it appears that the enemy is on the way, and closing in on us. We should see them within hours. Stay frosty and alert. The basement is our anticipated point of egress. You copy that, Sands?"

"Yes, sir," came the response.

Bridge could tell the soldier was nervous, but Bridge also knew he would stay his post. "Sands, you and the men with you have one simple order: anything opens that door, you unleash hell on it."

"Sir, yes, sir." Came the reply, more confident now.

"Bridge, out." Bridge sat and waited. On the right side of the desk was the M-4, on the left the shotgun. Tonight, Bridge hoped his men could keep the wolves from breaking through the gate, but he had a sinking feeling that they would be crashing through.

Part 5: Fenrir & Ragnarok

The F-16s flew to their ordered coordinates and dropped the napalm strapped to their bellies. It lit up the darkness and consumed the forest where it landed. A small number of the werewolf pack was consumed, but the fire began to spread out into all directions, gorging itself on the forest.

Time passed as the men became anxious and nervous; every minute brought the danger closer. The initial adrenaline rush they had felt was giving way to fatigue. Jack sat with Emera, Ruby and the rest of the students in the auditorium. He liked the reassuring weight of the shotgun against his leg, and he took some comfort at the .38 in the waistband of his jeans; he had acquired a holster for the M-9 he had taken from Jonas. It tugged at his belt but was easier to carry rather than both pistols in his waistband. The fear and excitement, which lay at the outer edges of his thoughts, was trying to force its way into the foreground of his mind. Only through great effort was he able to keep it under control. Looking around, Jack noticed that Canva was the only soldier who looked as alert as he had when the guard duty started. Canva was just as alert but only because he had played the waiting game with the monster before and he was no longer scared of dying or feared the oncoming battle. He was a soldier; battle and death were his constant companions.

In the forest, the pack began to crawl up from the caverns they had been traveling through. A portion of the werewolves stayed in the caverns, seeking to enter through the cellar while most went toward the front of the school right into the kill zone the soldiers had created. Some still came around the school in a flanking maneuver to come upon the rear of the buildings that comprised the academy. The spark that had fired inside the Friedkin wolf's mind confounded the animal that controlled the body, but the orders had been given to the lesser wolves, and they would obey.

Jones sat alert in his perch, scanning the yard in front of him and, waiting. Royston was fighting off sleep as his eyelids fluttered up and down. Then without warning, the night lit up as two of the claymores went off. Howls of pain erupted as the claymores threw ball bearings and silver at the enemy. Jones could see the targets as they were burning, but the fire was not the killing factor; the werewolves were ripping into their own bodies trying to remove the silver, not knowing the silver had melted from the explosion and was coursing into their bodies. Royston startled awake and looked on in horror as he saw a werewolf rip open its own stomach and begin tearing out organs. The werewolf then stumbled into the tripwire for another claymore and detonated it. The blast, ball bearings, and silver put the beast down, and it did not move again. After the initial howls died, the remainder of the pack lurking in the woods rushed forward through the area, which had been cleared of mines. The soldiers opened fire, the rounds making contact and forcing the werewolf bodies to jerk with the impact of each bullet. Jones smiled; his time had come at last.

Chambering the first round in the belt of ammunition, he opened fire, and werewolves were blown into pieces as the .50 caliber machine gun tore through them. Limbs were separated from bodies, and heads were completely destroyed, and still the beasts came rushing into the gap.

In the cellar, Sands and the men with him sat watching the door as the explosions and gunfire started. Then, they heard the thud from the other side of the door that led into the cave system. He waited and prepared to fire the mounted gun. Something was running fast on the other side of the door, because when it hit the iron door, it ripped the top hinge out of the stone and dented the door. Sands did not wait to identify the enemy or confirm what it was. Bridge had given him specific orders. The werewolf that stood in the hallway glared at the men that stood between it and the staircase to the main floor. Other werewolves were coming through the dented door. Sands pressed the trigger and opened fire. The first invader that had torn the door from the wall was dead within the first ten shots. The second fell even quicker, and by the time Sands let off of the trigger, he had used all the ammunition in the box and had to reload. Fortunately, the bodies of the dead made a good barricade with the door having been pulled free. From the other side of the carcasses came sounds of snarling and digging. Sands replaced the ammo box as quickly as he could and prepared to open fire.

The individuals in the auditorium heard the explosions on the lawn and then heard the gunfire, followed by gunfire from within the house. Jack remained calm; until they were compromised in the room, there was nothing he could do.

Sergeant Tuskman was on the roof, giving orders to the soldiers on the ground. He was using night vision binoculars to make sure that the flanks were not attacked. While he was concentrating on the frontal assault, he never noticed the shadow that climbed onto the roof of the wing of the house toward the rear of the compound. This shape stayed close to

163

Friedkin's Curse

the shingles on the roof and tried to stay out of Tuskman's line of sight. Tuskman did see it, but it was too late. The werewolf had already made it over the railing onto the observation deck where Tuskman had taken up his post. Bringing the M-4 to bear, Tuskman spoke into his microphone: "Rooftop breach," was all he said.

He fired six rounds into the monster's thick muscular chest before his jaw was ripped completely off of his face and the upper part of his skull was smashed in. His death was so quick that he never felt the claws cut his flesh or his brain destroyed by the fragments of his skull being driven into it.

Sergeant Wiine had heard the message Tuskman had put out and ran to the chapel door. Peering out, he looked down the corridor toward the far end of the hall where the rooftop stairway was. Three werewolves came bounding down the hallway. The lead werewolf locked eyes with Wiine. The sergeant ran out the chapel door as the werewolves hit the tripwire left in the hallway. The lead werewolf made it through but the other two were caught in the explosions from the detonating grenades. The shrapnel and power of the explosion liquefied several of their internal organs and tore out massive chunks of muscle.

Wiine reached the third floor landing and made sure that he was clear of the stairway so that the grenades would not catch him when they went off. The surviving werewolf had a tan color to its fur and stood watching Wiine. He drew his sidearm as the werewolf snarled; it tensed its shoulders, and Wiine shot straight into the legs of the beast. It fell onto the first wire, causing the grenades to explode and propelling the creature into a flying somersault. When it landed, it fell on the second wire near the rail where a grenade had been placed. When it detonated, the werewolf was blown apart where it lay. Wiine watched it blow the fiend's chest out completely and then tear the beast apart at the seams. The stairs were gone, as had been the plan all along. Wiine turned his back to keep the smoke out of his eyes and reached for his microphone. Something hit his back and sent him sprawling to the ground. Then, he felt the skin and muscles of his back being ripped apart. He tried to scream and reach behind him to stop the pain. He felt a sharp pain then his hand went numb; when he pulled his arm back around, his hand had been ripped off just below the wrist.

The werewolf that had jumped across the gap left by the destroyed stairs continued tearing into the sergeant until he reached the liver, at which point he dug in with his muzzle, tore the organ out, and ate it. Standing on the fourth floor landing was the werewolf that Jack and Owen encountered on their first night, the one that Bridge had hunted and that his men referred to as Hostile Zero. The one that had once been General Friedkin. Lifting his snout into the air, he breathed deeply, picking up the pheromones that had kept him near this place. So it was that he waited with his forces near the top of the building; the time to strike would be soon, and when it was, he would know it.

Bridge was aware of the gunfire surrounding his position and stood up to look out the window. He thought to himself about the day he had been given this mission, how easy he had thought the task at hand would be. It had proved to be anything but, and now he was here just as Custer had been. The orange glow on the horizon drew Bridge from his inner thoughts. He knew it was the fires started by the napalm; it would consume the forest, the town of Mead's hall, and the school. All evidence would be erased by the purifying flames.

Friedkin's Curse

Sands watched as the bodies piled in front of the door toppled over and more werewolves tried to come through only to be met by the heavy rounds of his M-249. He fired until the chamber clicked empty, then two of the three men assigned to help him guard the door would open fire. The other man always faced the door down into the cellar. The werewolves started coming forward despite the gunfire being poured into them. One would drop and the others would step over the fallen body. It was terrifying just how much damage they would take before dropping. Reloading his M-249, Sands began firing into the encroaching mass of fangs and fur. They began falling back. The men at his sides reloaded their weapons and waited. Sands did not want to alarm them, but he only had two more boxes of ammunition, then he'd be resorting to an M-4 he had acquired. At that point, the cellar would be overrun. He watched as the invaders retreated once again through the door. Their progress forward could be traced by the bodies lying along the hallway. Once werewolves, they had now retaken their original forms of men, women, and in a few cases children. Once the last figure disappeared into the darkness beyond the doorway, Sands quit firing. He knew there would be another rush; it was just a question of when.

Jones watched as the werewolves coming onto the lawn began to diminish; what had started as a flood of hostile forces had slowed to a trickle. He smiled as he took a break to reload his .50 caliber and let the barrel cool down. Royston handed up another box of ammunition to Jones. Royston was relieved because he had not had to fire a single shot so far; between Jones' .50 caliber and the men guarding the main entrance, everything coming across the lawn had been effectively handled, without his participation. All reports coming in sounded like it was under control:

the cellar was being kept clear, and the roof had been disabled thanks to the grenade traps the men had set, the lawn was the major concern, and it appeared that there were no more werewolves waiting to attack.

Then, Royston heard the men by the door scream and begin firing. Jones saw it first; one of the beasts had scaled the truck parked nearest them and jumped directly into the middle of the formation. The damage was immediate; the men broke rank trying to flee the werewolf. Royston leaned his head out the window and saw men racing toward him. He ducked his head back inside and laid in the floorboard hoping nothing would notice him. Jones cursed under his breath; he could not get a clear shot. Neither could the men. Jones saw at least five friendly fire incidents, watching as men fleeing were shot by the soldiers on the other side of the werewolf.

Finally, one of the men who had been assigned a shotgun was able to put a round right into the back of the werewolf's head, but too late. Before the body hit the ground the remainder of the pack in the woods swarmed forward. The men were not going to be able to reform ranks. Some took up firing positions where they stood and others tried to get back to formation. Neither option worked. Jones opened up on the front lawn; he had no shortage of targets. The men who had taken to firing at the werewolves were overrun as soon as the enemy reached them. A few were able to take out a werewolf or two. The men running back to form ranks were overtaken before getting close to the door. One of the soldiers pulled a pin on a grenade before falling. The explosion blew several werewolves into the sky, limbs missing. Royston looked on and saw what was happening and knew they had to fall back. "Jones, we need to go." Royston said.

Friedkin's Curse

Jones just shot Royston a bird. He opened the door facing the brick exterior of the building and ran toward the doors. Several of the men were still there and firing into the oncoming mass. Jones was laughing as the bullets left his machine gun and decimated the enemy. All semblance of reason had left him. Finally, a white werewolf jumped into the Humvee, and Jones felt the tug at his leg. He pulled a grenade from his pocket, pulled the pin, and waited.

The werewolf jerked him through the opening with such force that the whiplash knocked the grenade from his hand. It fell from the roof and landed under the Humvee. Jones smelled the blood on his attacker's breath, and then the grenade went off and flipped the Humvee over onto its top. Jones was now on top of the monster. He pulled his sidearm and unloaded the entire magazine into the monstrous face. It quit moving, and Jones breathed a sigh of relief, then several pairs of claws pulled him from the wreckage and tore him limb from limb.

Royston watched from the steps leading into the building. The man who had taken charge out front ordered the men to drop grenades and retreat. Each of the men dropped one grenade and ran inside the building. The grenades detonated sending a wave of death and dismemberment into the front wave of attack. Then, the commanding officer pulled a detonator from his pocket and depressed the red button on top of it. There were several explosions as the plastic explosives detonated, knocking the columns away. With a great rending sound, the roof over the door fell the four stories and blocked the entrance, crushing werewolves as it landed. Royston and the survivors from the front lawn went to the auditorium, which Royston began thinking of more and more as the Alamo.

The snipers had fired until their rifles were out of ammunition. Now they merely surveyed the scene, relaying battlefield news to Bridge and Canva. When the werewolf on the third floor caught their scent, it stalked the men, smelling sweat, leather, and gunpowder. The first man did not see or hear death sneak up on him, then in one mighty swipe it ripped his head loose, only a few pieces of vein and spine keeping the head from falling onto the floor. Going next door, the werewolf sank its fangs into the man's throat, crushing his spine and windpipe inside its massive jaws. The man lay on the floor suffocating as the werewolf made its way to the other end of the hall.

Before it reached the remaining snipers, the man had died. The third sniper started to turn when it heard the click of a claw on the tiled floor. In mid-turn, he was lifted and thrown into the wall. The beast unleashed a fury of blows on the man, rupturing several internal organs before finally ripping through the front of his skull. When the third sniper had been thrown into the wall, it alerted the fourth man, who had shut the door to his room and drew his sidearm.

He waited patiently and relayed the information to Canva and Bridge that the building was compromised on the third floor. He took off the microphone and waited, sidearm pointed toward the door. The door splintered and the man opened fire, putting two where the heart would be and one into the head. Before he could squeeze the trigger again, the beast had crossed the room and ripped the man's forearms from his body. He saw the bloody bone protruding where his elbow had been, but the pain had not hit him, and it never would. A slight smile came upon his lips as he saw the small red mark where his bullet had hit the werewolf between the eyes. It had bounced off of the incredibly thick bone that comprised the transformed skull. The werewolf had no such problem penetrating the

169

Friedkin's Curse

man's skull with his claws. Feeling rage at the small pain the man had caused overwhelmed the monster as he rendered the man a ragged pile of raw meat.

Canva listened to the message as the men from the lawn came into the auditorium. Royston reported the status of the door to the lieutenant. This information was relayed to Bridge by Canva, though it made little difference, as the pack was obviously in the building on the floors above them, waiting. "Canva," Jack said, "what's going on?"

"We have a last-stand scenario." Canva thought for a second and then divulged all the tactical information he had.

"So, the front door is blocked, the cellar is holding, but we have werewolves upstairs?" Jack asked.

Canva nodded. Jack walked back to Emera who was sitting in a chair by Ruby in the middle of a large huddle of students. She looked up at Jack, seeking some glimmer of hope. He met her eyes and tried to force a confident smile. Emera was not fooled. The anxiety that lay like a lead weight in her stomach increased. The children sensing the mood in the room and seeing the soldiers coming in were getting more nervous. Some of them were starting to cry. "Hey," Jack said, getting their attention. "It's going to be all right."

He walked over toward Canva once again and stood beside the man, neither one saying anything just listening and waiting.

Sands had forced another charge back and began loading his second to last ammunition box onto the M-249, the two men at his side firing intermittently into the doorway, trying to keep the horde back. Slamming down the cover, he primed the bolt and opened fire, keeping the danger at bay when he heard a new sound. It was the sound he'd feared hearing all night. The M-249 had jammed. "Shit, shit, shit!" He said as he scrambled to get the cover off and clear the jam.

The men at his side took back up their firing, but the werewolves could sense the trouble and came pouring into the cellar. Sands knew he'd never get the jam cleared in time. Detonating the explosives in the cave, he picked up the M-4 and began firing three-round bursts into the attackers, aiming at their legs. They were slowed as the front lines continued to stumble and fall until the explosives caused a cave in, forming a barricade while trapping other werewolves underneath it. After dispatching the remaining creatures, Sands gave the order to fall back, leaving the jammed M-249; with the debris blocking the werewolves, he and his men were afforded a quick withdraw without having to outrun the quick beasts, a feat which at this distance would have nearly been impossible.

The men emerged from the cellar into the hallway, where a nervous private stood watch outside of Bridge's door. The young man was sweating horribly, his M-4 held in front of him at the ready. The private informed Sands and his men of the situation. Tentatively, Sands knocked on the door. "General, sir." He said.

"Come in."

Sands opened the door and saw Bridge sitting behind the desk, his hands folded in front of him. "Sir," Sands began, "we've lost the cellar. We've formed a barricade that'll slow down the hostiles, but we have to head to the fallback point."

Bridge shook his head. "This is my fallback point."

"Permission to take your guard and meet up with the main force in the auditorium, sir."

"Permission granted."

Sands saluted and went back into the hallway. "Come on," he said to the private. "You've been relieved."

The private's face lit up with relief at having been pulled from what was seen as a suicide duty. As they made their way to the foyer to cross and go to the auditorium, a shadow moved on the ground near the foyer doorway. Holding up his hands, Sands stopped the men. The shadow stayed on the ground, not moving. It was just another shadow, but Sands was positive that it had moved. With hand signals, Sands conveyed his thoughts on the possible danger.

He took up a position against the far side of the wall and in a crouch began moving down the hallway while the other four men waited, their weapons aimed ahead. Well out of eyesight of the foyer, Sands aimed and let off a three round burst at the corner of the sheet rock, the lurking killer was peppered with the rounds and splinters from the wall. It moved out where Sands could see it, and he ran back to the men. Shaking off the irritation in its back, the monster came into the hallway. "Down!" Screamed one of the men.

Sands dove onto the floor as all four soldiers opened fire on the werewolf. The fiend dropped dead onto the floor in a heap. Still on the ground, Sands looked behind him at the abomination, then stood up and went back to the group of men. "There may be more out there." He told them.

As if on cue, two more werewolves came rushing down the hall. The men opened fire, but their magazines emptied before they could bring down the beasts. Sands was thrown over the group from his place in front as the monsters rushed to reach the cluster of men. He landed hard on his shoulder and knee, causing a sprain in both. Trying to stand, he fell, as the screams of the men filled the hall. Using the M-4 as a crutch he was able to stand and leaned against the wall as he fed a fresh magazine into the rifle. He watched as the men were mauled. One of the soldiers stumbled back holding his severed arm in his hand. "Sands..." he mumbled before he was pulled back among the slaughtered men.

The halls were splattered with blood, and the floor resembled that of a slaughterhouse instead of a school. Sands hobbled back to the door and saw the werewolves looking at him, blood and bits of the men falling from their mouths as they licked the gore from their teeth and came toward him. He opened the door and fell in, kicking the door closed. Sitting up, he turned the lock as the door shook and tipped a nearby bookcase over in front of the door, for an extra obstacle, ignoring his burning shoulder. Bridge still sat behind the desk but the M-4 was in his hand and pointed at the door. Sands hobbled back toward the desk. "That should hold them for a little bit." He sat on the desk and noticed the shotgun behind it. "The others are dead."

Bridge nodded. "Tie up that knee. It'll give you a little more stability."

Sands ripped a piece of his uniform off and wrapped it tightly around his knee. It would help to keep the swelling down and make the pain more manageable. "Sir, this situation is FUBAR."

Bridge nodded again. He laid the M-4 on the desk and went over to the bookcase on the other side of the door and tipped it over in front of the other one. "Every little bit helps." He said to Sands.

Sands was scared now; in the cellar, it had seemed like they had a chance. Little had he known that the school had already been compromised. He checked the magazine in the M-4 and then the remaining magazines in his ammo pouch. "Top drawer, right side." Bridge said. Opening the drawer, Sands saw that it was filled with

Friedkin's Curse

magazines. "We should probably lay them all out on the desktop; when they breach, we'll need them quick."

Sands agreed and emptied his ammo pouch onto the desktop and then began taking the magazines out of the desk drawer and laying them beside his magazines, trying to make even rows. Looking out the large window in the rear of the office, Sands saw the long narrow path of the cave-in that he had detonated. He let out an appreciative whistle. "Closed that door," he said to himself.

The men in the auditorium had heard the gunfire from down the hallway. Jack sat beside Emera and handed her the .38. "Remember at the range?" He asked. She nodded. "Good, same rules apply. If it gets past the soldiers, aim for the head." He started to go back to the line of soldiers to help them when needed but stopped a few steps away and came back. "Almost forgot." He said, retrieving two leather pouches that would normally be attached to a belt.

She opened the first pouch and saw six more bullets. "What are these for?" She asked.

"Just in case." He said. Jack grabbed Emera and kissed her, relishing the feel of her lips. "Stay with your sister." He said to Ruby.

Ruby just shook her head and nuzzled deeper into Emera's side. Jack walked back to the soldiers. "What's going to happen?" Ruby asked Emera.

"I don't know." She told her young sister honestly.

"Are we going to be okay?"

Emera gave her sister a smile. "You see that guy?" She asked, pointing to Jack. Ruby's mouth turned up into a smile. "I feel sorry for anything that tries to get in here to hurt us."

"Yeah," Ruby said, easing the death grip she had on Emera's waist.

Emera was positive that Jack would do everything possible to keep her and Ruby safe, but she wasn't as confident in their odds. Soldiers had come in from the lawn, and with the gunfire from inside the building, they knew that at least some of the werewolves were in the school.

The soldiers kept their eyes on the doors to the auditorium, poised and ready. It was the best option they had for a choke point. They knew once the sun was up they only had to worry about Hostile Zero. Were they to be near a window, they would see the flames licking up the forest encroaching ever closer to the school, but even the imminent threat of the fire would not register against the much more immediate threat inside the building with them.

Most of the students were watching the doors as well. They were not sure of what was going on, but the soldiers attitudes were telling them that something was wrong. Everyone was so intent on the door that no one paid attention to the small scratching sound. Emera thought she saw something in her peripheral vision; she turned her head and did not see anything. She waited and saw it again. Dust was falling down from the ceiling. "Jack!" Jack and Canva turned in time to see Emera hurry the kids against the wall and away from the spot where the dust had come from. "The ceiling," she said, pointing up.

Jack looked up and saw the dust falling from the ceiling. "They're digging through," Canva said from behind him.

The soldiers quickly turned away from the door and looked at the ceiling where small pieces of plaster had replaced the dust and descended to the floor of the auditorium. Then, without warning, a pair of muscular arms burst through the ceiling and tore a massive hole in it. "Fire!" Canva ordered.

The men opened fire, and a bloody bullet-riddled body fell to the auditorium floor. It hit with a thud and began to shift back into a human shape. One of the students screamed. Some of the men looked toward the ceiling, expecting to see another werewolf, and the others looked toward the door. At the door stood one of the monsters, the one that had escaped the school the night before, the one they believed to have been Simone. The men fired on her and cut her down in a moment. Royston, who was on the end of the formation of men, looked around, trying to find the easiest escape route should the need arise. He had no idea where he would run to, but he was sure the stage had storage facilities beneath it.

As the creature by the door fell to the ground, there was a thud behind the soldiers. They spun in time to see a werewolf standing in the middle of the auditorium. It lunged into the hail of gunfire the soldiers were laying down. Jack was the only one, who had not fired a shot. He was aware of the limitation of his weapon. The beast dropped, near Jack and rose only to have Jack blow a hole in its chest. A few of the soldiers put some rounds into the head to make sure it stayed down. Jack took a quick glance back toward the door, but there was no sign that an attack would come from that direction.

Several forms lunged through the hole in the ceiling, aiming at specific targets. Two of them landed on top of small groups of soldiers while one landed in front of a cluster. The ones that were landed on never had a chance. With the weight and momentum of the werewolf, if it hit a man, it broke several bones. The crunches echoed in the auditorium and then the screams followed. The one that landed in front of the soldiers was shot dead, but not before it was able to kill at least three men. Two died instantly as their chests were smashed to pulp by ferocious blows, the other lay on the ground trying to put his small intestine back inside the mangled flesh of his stomach.

The soldiers were firing on the small invading force and even managed to take down two of them before the next wave came crashing down and ran toward the soldiers, rushing through them, and scattering their firepower. "Form ranks!" Canva ordered from the chaos as he fired point blank into the snarling jaws of a werewolf. The beast dropped dead at his feet. "Watch your fire!"

Royston giggled to himself. "This is a cluster fuck." He said to no one in particular.

He dropped his M-4 and ran toward the stage; the students and Emera saw what was happening and screamed at every wound they saw inflicted. Royston ran by them, drawing the attention of a nearby werewolf, which went after the escaping soldier. Royston pulled open the small doors facing the audience at the bottom of the stage, stepped in and turned to close the doors when the heavily muscled body of the pursuing monster slammed into him, sending him crashing further into the darkness. His screams rose above the din of the battle raging in the enclosed auditorium. The werewolf emerged from the small enclave slicked with blood, and in the darkness laid the remains of Royston. Most medical professionals would not recognize the mass of sinew and bone that had been Royston as having once been human.

Sands and Bridge sat on the desk, watching the door when they heard the gunfire coming from the auditorium. Bridge sighed and shook his head. Then, the brass handle on the door rattled. Sands watched amazed as the handle turned and the door tried to move against the heavy burden of the bookcases. With a loud screech, the heavy oak cases began to scratch the hardwood floor as they began to move. Sands moved as fast as he could to the side of the blockade and fired through the crack in the door until the weight against the door disappeared and the door moved back into its place.

The click of the handle helped to relieve him somewhat. Then, the door pushed in harder and more fervently this time. Sands fired until his M-4 clicked empty. He discarded the used magazine and turned as Bridge tossed him another one. Slamming the magazine in as he had been taught, he chambered the first round and fired until the magazine was empty. Again, Bridge threw him another magazine; Sands slammed it home and waited to fire. The force pushing the door seemed to have stopped, but the door did not close as it had before. Cautiously, Sands looked out the crack between the door and the doorframe. Slumped against the oak were two werewolves shifting back into their human guises. Sands could make out shadows moving in the hallway but could not get a count.

He stepped back to the desk. "Two down, and I don't know how many more waiting out there." He told Bridge.

Bridge leaned on the corner of the desk, the M-4 held at his side. "As many as it takes." He said.

Sands kept watch as a fur-covered, clawed hand reached through the crack and gripped the door. He raised the rifle to his shoulder and took aim when the fingers exploded. From the hallway came a howl of pain, and Sands looked over and saw the smoke coming out the end of Bridge's M-4. Bridge once again lowered his rifle beside him. The door was splintered where the bullets had bitten into it, and blood marked the spot. Sands was feeling better about the odds of being stuck in the room with Bridge.

Jack watched as more werewolves came down the hole in pairs and the soldiers were being slaughtered and scattered. Running through the center of the room to the far wall, Jack took Emera by the hand. "We've got to get out of here. If we can get into a room, I think I can hold them off. Make sure the kids are ready to run." He told her. She just nodded.

Jack led the way around the room, picking up Royston's M-4 as he went when a soldier's upper torso was thrown into the wall in front of them. Jack bent and retrieved his ammo belt and several grenades from the man. They made their way through the room as the soldiers tried to stand their ground against the werewolves. Canva stood in the middle of the soldiers, giving orders and firing into the fur-covered invaders.

It seemed the men had their fear under control now and were working as a cohesive unit. From the rear of the werewolves, Jack spotted three beasts breaking off from the main assault and running toward them. He let the shotgun drop on its sling to his waist and used the M-4 to take the charging monsters down. He fired bursts of shots into their legs and arms, immobilizing them temporarily. With the werewolves rebuilding their joints and muscles, Jack fired three-shot bursts into their foreheads. The impact of the bullets made the werewolves fall over and they began to change back to human. Sliding the sling of the M-4 over his other shoulder, Jack let it drop and took back up his shotgun.

"Jack," he heard Canva call. Jack turned toward the man. "They're all over the building. This is still the safest room."

Jack shook his head and pointed above them. "Smaller quarters, less room for surprise." He yelled back to Canva.

With the creatures pressing harder on the soldiers, Canva had to turn his full attention back to the problem at hand. Jack could see out the door and did not see any sign of an ambush. He took several large steps

Friedkin's Curse

ahead of the group and dove through the door, coming up in a crouch and pointing the shotgun one way and then the other. When he cleared the door way, he scanned the foyer, making sure that there were no surprises waiting for them. He could see the mangled remains of the front door with portions of the blockade having pushed through and heard the furious sounds of digging coming from the other side. There were other noises coming from down the hallway, but they were not his concern.

Emera and the students followed closely behind him, Emera's finger never leaving the trigger of the .38. Watching closely near the second-floor landing, Jack was aware that there were sounds coming from above them, but he could not be sure just what floor. They looked at the landing ahead of them and did not see any threats. Jack opened the door for the others to go through. "Find a classroom, the smaller the better." Jack told Emera.

"I know just the one," Ruby said, pulling Emera by the hand.

The other students quickened their pace to keep up. Jack heard the wood of the third-floor landing being carved and realized where the sounds he had heard were coming from. No werewolves had tried to pursue from the ground floor because the majority were already congregated on the third. As the students continued by, Jack took two of the grenades he had taken off of the dead soldier, and pulled the pins. He counted to two and threw them up over the rail near the top of the stairs in front of the third-floor landing. They detonated and sent the stairs crashing down. With the slight buzzing in his ears, Jack did not hear the rustle until the screams erupted. The last few students were trying to get into the door when one of the fiends swung down from the third floor landing.

Three of the young girls were swept up in its massive arms, and it turned to flee. Jack raised the shotgun, and the werewolf rushed past, kicking Jack. Jack was thrown back into the door, cracking it. Had the shotgun not been on a sling it would have went flying out of his grasp; the last Jack saw, the beast leaped off of the landing, ignoring the stairs with three girls in its arms. The one that Jack could see was a little redheaded girl with hazel eyes. Tears were streaming down her face, and her arm was stretched out toward Jack. Hobbling while his lungs refilled with air, Jack looked over the railing and all sign of the werewolf was gone. Jack could hear the screams of the girls as it was lost amidst the gunfire. He stumbled through the door and knelt on the cold tile floor. Tears fell from his eyes as he remembered the fear on the face of the child.

Standing up and wiping his eyes, Jack went to the classroom with the others. Some of the students were crying and others had cried until the tears ran dry. Emera sat in a desk against the back wall. "Everybody," Jack said getting their attention, "we need to start piling up desks."

With the help of the students, Jack had most of the desks piled near the door. Not as a barricade but as an obstacle, the ceiling was too low for the werewolves to clear the desks in a leap, so they would have to climb over or try to push it over. Either way, they would provide him with a much better target than if they had freedom of movement. Everyone sat against the back wall, huddled together, and at the epicenter of them all were Emera and Ruby. Jack stood watching. He was looking at the ceiling tiles in case dust fell or one of them was disturbed and he noticed the walls in case they were trying to be broken into. He knew the creatures were waiting, and there were still several hours left until sunrise.

Canva and the men had repelled the werewolves. The soldiers had taken heavy casualties at first but had quickly overcome the situation. With the remaining werewolves having escaped, Canva felt it best to try and find a more secure location. He could not raise Bridge, which concerned him. If something happened to the general, then he would be chief ranking officer; it would be his command. "All right, men, we need to move upstairs. The civilians have been taken upstairs, so we will attempt to find them and resume our mission to guard them."

The men were cautious entering the hallway, not wanting to be surprised by anymore attacks. What they found was much worse. On the far side of the foyer sat a monster devouring the chest cavity of a girl, one of the students. It looked up at the men, the tiny, fist-sized heart dangling by the veins from its fangs. With a quick snap, the heart was gone, eaten by the beast. "Kill it." Whispered one of the soldiers.

One of the privates fired on the murderous thing. The beast was dead with the first six shots in its skull, which did not stop the soldier from emptying the entire thirty-round magazine into the carcass. Taking the stairs two at a time, the soldiers ran up the flight and saw the cracked door and the demolished stairs. Canva sent two men down each direction from the landing, not sure which way the civilians had gone. One of the men emerged through the cracked door with a smile on his face. "We found them." He said.

Canva looked down the other direction to call back the men, but they were not there. He thought he saw an M-4 lying on the hallway. "Get to the room, double time." He ordered as he covered their progress from the rear.

A werewolf exited the room at the other end of the hallway and stood snarling at the men. Canva watched as it merely stood and waited. Then, when the men were at the door to the room where the civilians waited, it let loose a howl that rattled the window panes. Forms began dropping down from above. Even though they were falling and stayed out of sight, Canva knew what they were. "Firing positions, across the hall." The men scrambled to take up a position to repel a full-frontal assault.

Bridge and Sands stood behind the desk, having kept the door closed and intact despite several tries from the werewolves to get inside. From above them came a fearsome howl, causing the windows to rattle. A renewed banging came on the door, only this time it sounded different. Almost like claws on wood as opposed to fists. The door shook but not as violently as before. Then, it became apparent to Bridge, who fired into the middle of the door; Sands stared at his superior officer. "They're clawing through it." He explained. Sands joined him in firing into the door.

No matter how many rounds they fired, it did no good and the sounds of scratching grew louder and more frenzied the longer it continued until they punched a hole through the door and a fur-covered wolf snout entered and sniffed. Bridge walked as close to the door as he could and opened fire. The snout was destroyed, and from the other side came the sounds of the angry pack. They began enlarging the hole in the door, unveiling more and more of them. Bridge dashed back to the desk and picked up the shotgun. He began firing into the exposed targets, but it was too many. They ignored the wounded and the dead and continued working on the door, trying to gain access. Bridge knew it was only a matter of minutes before they were dead. He took a grenade in each hand. "Get behind the desk and take cover." He ordered Sands.

Sands obeyed, taking cover behind the desk, and covered his head with his hands. Bridge pulled the pins and tossed the grenades through the holes in the door into the horde of monsters trying to get to them. He turned to rush back to the desk, but one of the grenades detonated early. The concussive wave threw Bridge over the desk and into the window, the

Friedkin's Curse

glass broke but the bars held. Bridge fell to the floor, minor cuts on his back and neck, a wooden spike protruding from his shoulder. Sands assumed it was debris from the door; he pulled the general under the desk with him and checked Bridge's pulse. It was strong and steady; the man was only unconscious. Sands rose up and looked over the desk. Where the door had been was now a giant, gaping hole, blood, bone, fur and muscle lay around the destruction and even covered the front of the desk. The explosion was still ringing in his ears, so Sands kept a watchful eye on the enlarged entryway. The floor was depressed and sagging, but might hold their weight when it was time to evacuate or the weight of an attacking monstrosity.

Jack and the others sat in the room, listening to the orders being given out in the hallway when the wall on the far side of the room crumbled and collapsed as an explosion occurred underneath them. The floor began to sag on that side of the room. "Stay away from that." Jack cautioned. Howls came from the other end of the hall and gunfire erupted from right outside the door. "Everybody down," Jack ordered as he approached the door in a crouch, the M-4 at the ready.

He opened the door and peered around the frame. Dozens maybe even hundreds of werewolves were pouring in from the landing and the soldiers were pouring fire into them. Beasts at the front of the procession would fall dead, only to have the encroaching creatures swarm over them. Jack turned back to the girls. "Where's the science room?"

"Next door." One of the girls screamed with tears streaming down her face.

"Is it connected to another room?" The girl nodded her head. "How many?"

"Two," she said

"Good, let's go." Jack led them next door and told them to go through the doors connecting to the farthest classroom.

Jack then turned on the gas hookups against the interior and rear walls and smelled the gas being pumped into the room. Running to Canva, Jack explained his plan. "No shooting, though."

"Fall back," Canva ordered as Jack led the men into the science room, pointing to the door on the far end.

He cautioned each of them not to discharge their weapon. Canva was the last to fall back. He and Jack slammed the door and sprinted to the connecting doorway, running across the vacant classroom to the room on the far end of the hallway where the students had taken refuge. Canva retrieved a flare from his vest, pulled the flint top off of it, and prepared to light it. The door did not hold for a second as the horde of werewolves came in and saw the men fleeing. They charged.

With one strike, Canva lit the flare and tossed it over the heads of the approaching werewolves. Jack and Canva dove to the floor as one of the soldiers closed the door. The flare ignited the gas, and the explosion was small, but because the room was compact and filled with the monsters, it destroyed many of them instantly and set the remainder on the outskirts of the room ablaze. They flailed and howled until the oxygen in their lungs burned out and they fell, no more than a burning carcass. There were still werewolves in the hall and behind them all was Hostile Zero. He had caught the scent and identified the one putting it off. He would not stop. With a growl, he ordered the remaining creatures into the room and down the hall to scour the rest of the rooms. His orders were obeyed; the feral horde charged down the hall and ran past the charred remains of their brethren to the doorways around the now burning room.

The door leading to the hallway was torn apart the same time that the connecting doorway to the other classroom was burst in. The soldiers had prepared for this and the invading werewolves were met with gunfire. Bullets tore through them. Despite the firepower, the beasts inched ever forward. "We're losing ground," one of the soldiers called.

Jack ran to the firing squad and began firing the shotgun, removing monsters from the fight with each shot. "Shotguns." Ordered Canva.

With the one-word order, any soldier with a shotgun forsook their M-4 and began firing the pump-action shotguns. The monstrosities could not withstand the concussive force of the deadly, close-range shotguns. Turning, they retreated the way they had come. Some of the soldiers followed their retreat as far as the door. It was a deadly mistake. While Jack went to the rear of the room with Emera and the students, the soldiers who had followed the werewolves were met by a leaping fiend who ripped open their chests and stomachs before anyone could react. One soldier stood as his small intestine lay on the floor; turning, the soldier stepped on long strand of internal organ and the slick mess on the floor caused him to fall on his back. His body hit with a thud, and he did not move again. The beast leaped toward another group of soldiers, who opened fire. The fiend landed and rolled past them, the lifeless form shrinking and returning to its original form. "Stay away from the doors." Ordered Canva. "We stay in our fire teams and deal with them as they attempt to breach."

No one argued with the order, but Jack was sure that the werewolves had several more surprises for them. The soldiers' number had dwindled to less than fifteen, and they were left wondering who might be the next to die.

Sands stayed in his position behind the desk, the M-4 laying across the wood top, waiting for any sign of attack. The fire loomed closer and had encompassed several hundred acres of forest as it ate its way to the school. Local fire departments were already mobilizing trying to create fire blocks and evacuate their citizenry, but in Mead's Hall, no one was calling about the fire, nor was there anyone at the fire department to answer the silent phone lines. Taking a quick glimpse over his shoulder, Sands wondered which would kill him first: the fire or the werewolves. Neither was a pleasant way to go in Sands' opinion. "Wha' hap en?" Bridge asked in slurred speech as he gradually came back to consciousness.

"You took a blast over the desk. There's some shrapnel in your arm, but I'm not sure removing it is the best course." Sands had done everything he could to stabilize the shard of wood and trimmed it down to where it wasn't such a danger of being driven in further.

"Gimme my rifle." He said, reaching for his weapon.

Sands handed him the M-4, the shot gun had been thrown through one of the panes of glass. They both sat in silence, looking down the sights of their rifles and waiting for any sign of an attack. None came because the monsters below in the catacombs had already fled back the way they came and gathered on the lawn with the horde that was still out there. Without new orders from Friedkin, they did what their beastly minds told them to do.

The bodies of the dead were devoured, the bones snapped open, and the marrow drained. Finally, one of the werewolves had caught the scent of the people on the second floor and attempted to climb up the destroyed facade of the school. The first few to attempt it fell back with bits of brick grasped in their paws. More and more werewolves began

Friedkin's Curse

trying to climb the front of the building and found places where the damage was not a hindrance to the ascent. They tried to rip out the bars on the windows and found that they still held fast, so they climbed higher until they came to the roof and found an entrance.

Sands and Bridge were unaware of the dangers above them and waited on the dangers outside their door, the dangers that had already been destroyed. "Sir, do we have a way to get out of here?"

Bridge looked at the man, dazed and with unfocused eyes. "Yes." Bridge pulled a small notebook from his breast pocket. "Find the code and radio it in."

Bridge went back to watching the door, and Sands looked around fervently for the radio and the code that would call in an evacuation.

Canva inspected their inventory; they had a few grenades left and still enough ammunition to hold out for several hours. One soldier had found a small, three-stick bundle of dynamite in one of the dead soldiers' ammunition packs. Leaning out to where he could see, Canva watched the unsettling sight as the werewolves paced from empty room to empty room, waiting for something. Taking one of the grenades, he began to pull the pin when a hand clamped over his. It was Jack, and he was shaking his head. "Save them until we have a big enough crowd."

Canva nodded his agreement. The abominations disgusted him with their familiar humanity and otherworldly nature. "We've got to try and make a run for it." Canva said.

Jack shook his head. "We go out there, and you know they have the upper hand."

"We stay in here too longm and they have it then." Canva said just as a new group of werewolves came through the doors. "Shit." Canva mumbled under his breath.

"That's a good crowd," Jack said, nodding toward the small round object Canva held.

He pulled the pin and threw the grenade as far down the hall as he could get it. One of the creatures snarled before the grenade bounced once on the floor and then detonated. It put a dent in the front lines of the approaching pack. Then, Friedkin stepped out of one of the nearby rooms. "Hostile zero." Canva said with a strange reverence.

Jack raised his M-4 and started firing at the father of the horrors. He had recognized it from their first night at the school. There was no reverence for Jack, only a need for vengeance for all the death and destruction he had witnessed all because of that one being. The werewolf did not seem fazed by the bullets pelting its abdomen. With a howl, Friedkin stepped aside, and the werewolves rushed forward. The soldiers began to fire into the muscle and fur that swept toward them. Canva let another grenade fly over the initial advance into the reinforcing section. The detonation, made it easier to hold back the initial wave because they did not have the support of the column behind them pushing them forward. The grenades had also weakened the floor, causing some of the monsters to fall to the floor below.

Jack looked into the hallway to find Friedkin, but he could not amidst the chaos in the hall. Letting the soldiers step up to the door, Jack retreated, keeping his eyes on the door until he was standing beside Emera with the students cowering against the back wall. Their eyes met, and she knew that it would be okay; she could see the optimism in his eyes. Jack kissed her cheek, and she closed her eyes and leaned forward, not wanting

189

Friedkin's Curse

the contact to be broken. Pulling away, Jack checked the battle raging across the room.

With a great rending crash, a large, fur-covered arm crashed through the ceiling. Emera threw her arms up, and the claw grabbed onto her forearm. "Jack!" She screamed.

Jack saw it start to move and wrapped his arms around the muscular wolf arm. He could feel the corded muscles like iron. In a great sweeping arc, Jack was pulled upward smashing through the sheetrock on the ceiling and up through the hardwood flooring. Emera screaming as she was pulled up underneath him. Opening his grasp, Friedkin let Emera drop while continuing the arc of his arm and planting Jack into the wall. More sheet rock collapsed behind him and several of the studs cracked and splintered. The impact jarred Jack too much, his grip loosened, and for him, the world went black.

He regained consciousness before hitting the floor. He looked and saw the monster Friedkin had become approaching Emera. Jack was the distraction; Emera was the goal. Emera crawled backwards away from the beast that was leering at her. It moved distinctly, slowly, each movement methodical. Friedkin had done this before, and the beast that controlled his mind enjoyed the suffering it caused. Despite the broken ribs, and pain flaring in every muscle and nerve in his body, Jack found a greater force, something that overrode everything in his mind. It was primal, it was good, and it was rage. Standing with no thought to the pain, Jack's lungs exhaled in the scream of a madman. Friedkin stopped and turned. He recognized the sound for what it was: a challenge. "Back the fuck off, fluffy!" Jack screamed, spittle flying with each word.

Friedkin let loose his own answering cry and charged. The bloody man with bruises covering his back and sides rushed to meet the foe, shotgun ready. Friedkin leaped at Jack, Jack let those arms reach him and felt the pressure as the claws dug into his shoulders and pushed him over. Once he felt the butt of the shotgun meet the floor, he pulled the trigger and the shotgun erupted into Friedkin's stomach, carrying him over onto his back behind Jack. Jack rolled over and hopped to his feet. He pumped the weapon, the expended shell ejecting down into the hole they had made in the floor. Friedkin looked into his eyes, and Jack pulled the trigger.

Nothing happened. The gun was empty. Friedkin smiled in triumph, Jack screamed in frustration, and Emera cried in terror. Jack slammed the hard butt of the shotgun into Friedkin's face. Pain rippled through his features as the wood made contact with his snout, and Jack was rewarded with a satisfying crack as bone gave way. Raising the shotgun above his head to club the beast again, Jack grinned, a grin that would make anyone seeing know that this man had lost all reason. As the improvised club descended, Friedkin's hand shot up and caught the butt of the gun. The weapon was jerked from Jack's grasp. Ripping the barrel free from the stock, Friedkin rolled over and lunged into Jack. The massive shoulder caught him in the stomach, and Jack was tackled.

The werewolf was upon him. Saliva trickled down from the muzzle onto his face as he could hear the bones in its nose cracking back into place as they healed. Jack reached for anything of any use. Friedkin reared back and snapped down toward Jack's face with monstrous jaws. Jack found a piece of 2x10 that had been ripped up when they came crashing through the floor and grabbed it. Just as Friedkin was in range, Jack pushed the wood into the monster's gaping maw. The beast stopped as he tried to figure out what had happened. Without thinking, Jack reached down to his pocket and with a flick of his thumb opened his pocket knife and began stabbing into the side of Friedkin's head and neck. The

Friedkin's Curse

beast was still trying to deal with the 2x10. Finally, Jack hit the beast's bright amber eye and watched the blade dig into it, slicing open the cornea and plunging until the entire blade was embedded into that hideous eye. Friedkin turned and howled, the wood thrown from his mouth, the knife jammed through the eye socket and embedded into the skull itself. Friedkin tried to pull the blade free but could not; it was lodged too deep within the bone.

Anger filled the werewolf; the muscles stood out and shook with the anger that coursed through the demon's being. Jack remembered the pistol he had taken from Jonas and fired into the back of the werewolf. The bullets had no effect; the rage had taken away all concept of pain. The only thing that Friedkin wanted was to tear Jack limb from limb and then finish his conquest with Emera, but first, the man who stabbed him would pay. A large, clawed hand caught Jack in the shoulder and opened up his skin. Blood flowed from the wounds, and his shirt was soaking within seconds. Friedkin smelled the blood and licked his lips.

He came slowly toward Jack, realizing that he was no longer a threat, his weapons all gone, despite the one buried in his own eye. Jack, not caring about the danger yet realizing he would not be walking away from this fight, merely wanted to buy Emera as much time as possible, so he did the only thing he could think of and with the palm of his hand hit the bottom of the knife and sent a shockwave of pain through the entire skull of the beast. One backhand sent Jack onto the ground, blood pouring from his broken nose and split lips. This time the werewolf stood over Jack, reaching down and pulling him up by the front of his tattered shirt. Jack could smell the foul breath of the beast and knew this was the end.

Friedkin opened wide to bite into Jack's skull; Jack watched the mouth open into darkness and oblivion when he saw a silver wolf's head appear. Emera realizing Jack was moments away from death had snapped out of her terror and did the only thing she could think to. She had jumped onto Friedkin's back, using the wolf's head pendant and the chain as a bridle and reins. Friedkin pulled up in shock and tried to shake her off, but she dug in with her legs just as if she was riding a horse. The silver was doing nothing but keeping the werewolf from killing Jack. Seeing what was happening, Jack reached under Friedkin's arms and pulled the .38 from Emera's denim waistband. He pulled back the hammer and noticed that small ringlets of smoke had started to wisp up from the corners of Friedkin's mouth where the skin had been broken and the chain was making contact. "He's not immune; he's just got a tougher hide." Jack cried.

Emera pulled back on the chain, keeping Friedkin's face away from Jack. Taking careful aim with the eye that was not swollen shut, Jack waited. "Emera," he said loud enough for her to hear. "Let go when I say to."

"Are you crazy?"

"Do it ...NOW!"

Emera let go, and the release sent the werewolf's head forward, the pendant still in its mouth. The pendant slammed into the barrel of the .38, and Jack fired six shots, blowing the pendant into pieces and sending small slivers of silver shrapnel into the sinuses, skull, and throat of Friedkin. Jack squeezed the trigger three more times before he realized that the pistol was empty. He backed away from Friedkin, leading Emera by the arm. The werewolf stood still for a moment and then began to move. Smoke rose out of his nostrils and then he fell back to the floor, thrashing about. Jack took the ammunition pouch from her pocket and emptied the six shells into his hand. He loaded the new bullets into the pistol one-handed.

His right arm was useless after Friedkin had cut through muscle and damaged bone with his fury. Friedkin continued thrashing and standing up began to rip into his own throat and face. The claws dug into the throat, opened the jugular vein, and tore portions out of his nose and throat in attempts to claw out the silver. After a few more minutes of futility, he fell to the ground, still twitching. Jack pulled the knife free of the eye socket and cut open the beast's stomach. It was tough with the lean muscle but the knife did the job, pulling the skin apart. Jack could see the heart still pumping. "How?" Emera asked.

Jack then unloaded the revolver into the pumping mass of tissue until it was destroyed. It did not move or try to rebuild itself. Gradually, the skin began to melt away and the muscle deteriorated into gelatinous clumps on the floor as the skeleton shrunk, becoming a human skeleton lying in a puddle of goop that had once been a monster. A monster that terrorized and destroyed for over a hundred years. Emera wrapped her arms around Jack and tried not to squeeze him to hard. "Jack ..." Tears fell down her face. They were good tears, tears of relief and tears of joy.

"Love you, babe." He said, trying to smile but finding that almost every inch of his body was swollen and hurt.

"I love you."

The door to the room opened and several werewolves stood in the door. Jack turned and faced them. They looked at the clump on the floor and at Jack and then they cowered back and fled. The monsters, the only remainders of the invading force, fled onto the roof and into the forest. The sun would be up soon, and they would become human. In the forest, with the fire raging, they would be overtaken and destroyed by the oldest cleansing agent known to man. The fire still had some time before it would make an end to them. It still approached the school, the flames growing wider and hotter with every inch of ground they covered.

Part 6: Finished

"Hey!" Jack called into the hole in the floor. Several soldiers came running in, firing position toward Jack's call. "Need some help here."

"Where's it at?" Canva asked, stepping up near the destroyed sheetrock and plywood.

Jack kicked the brittle skeleton down to the next floor. It landed, and several of the bones cracked. Taking Emera by the hand, Jack lowered her down with his good arm until the soldiers had her, and Jack let go. Sitting down on the edge, Jack pushed off, making sure he stayed away from any jagged outcroppings. He hit and bent at the knees, but with the adrenaline gone from his system and his muscles pushed to the limits of endurance, he could not hold himself up and fell to the ground. Seeing the wounded shoulder, several of the soldiers took aim at Jack. Emera, Ruby, and several students ran in front of Jack. "What are you doing?" Emera demanded.

"Just procedure, ma'am," one of the soldiers said. "Sir?"

"They're right." Canva said. "Jack, what happened?"

"Claws and scratches. No bites." He said, feeling every muscle in his body ache and scream at him for the trials of the past few days. "Water?"

Canva pulled his canteen from his side and handed it to Emera. "Medic," Canva said to a soldier, who had a red cross taped onto his helmet. "Attend the man."

Emera poured the cold, refreshing water into Jack's mouth, and he relished the cool crispness of it. The medic took a look at the wound to

Friedkin's Curse

Jack's shoulder, and pulled a small sewing kit from his pack. "Morphine?" The medic asked.

Jack shook his head and was pleased to be conscious and have full function of his senses despite the pain the stitches caused him. Jack pointed out the window with his good hand. Canva saw the blaze as it ate through the trees. The brick structure of the school would prevent it from catching as quickly as the surrounding forest, but they would need to evacuate soon. Once the medic was through with him, Jack took stock of the people around him. There were several soldiers left, some lay sprawled into different positions near the door. Likewise, it seemed that there were fewer students than he remembered. Ruby and Emera hovered by his side as the medic set about stabilizing his wounds.

They left the classroom where they had made their final stand and started back toward the foyer of the first floor, watching their path to avoid falling through where the floor had been weakened. There were scattered bodies riddled with bullets through the hall. Men, women, and children lay nude and bloodied and all very dead. All of the somber survivors pitied the dead in the hallway and on the stairs, innocents turned into combatants against their will. The soldiers stayed on guard; Canva and another soldier took the lead while the other soldiers covered the rear. They did not find a werewolf. Jack did not expect them to after he witnessed the others run off. They were headed toward the hallway where Bridge had made his office. "General had a field radio." Canva explained to his men. "Let's hope it still works."

They saw the carnage outside the door and the gaping hole in the hall where the doorway had stood. Still alert and expecting danger to bound out at them, Canva peered carefully around the corner. When he turned back around to the men, he was smiling. "Sands! I'm coming in."

Stepping through the rabble of the former doorway, he saw the destroyed interior. Bridge, his face still pale, was sitting behind the desk, his back against the wall. Sands was standing behind the desk, cradling the M-4. The medic made his way to his commanding officer. With a few quick inspections, the medic turned back and gave a thumbs up to the men. "Where's the radio?" Canva asked. Sands pointed to the floor beside his feet. "We need to call for evac."

"I already did." Sands said, smiling and looking at his watch. "It should be here in twenty minutes."

Canva took a quick survey of Bridge and ordered two of the soldiers to tear down the curtains and make a sling to carry between them for Bridge to ride in. Bridge would occasionally mumble while this was occurring. The soldiers used one stick of dynamite to blow the bars out of the large window in the office. They exited the school and found the lawn pocked with craters and littered with bodies; the fire approached ever closer, now nearly toward the rear of the building. The group stared in shock at the carnage and combat that had raged on the front lawn. The soldiers formed a perimeter around the civilians, Jack leaning on Emera. Ruby with her friends stood clustered about them. "What's going to happen now?" Emera asked Jack.

Jack shrugged and then grimaced at the pain in his wounded shoulder. "They'll most likely give us some lecture about national security, make us sign waivers, and then let us go home."

Emera was so relieved to be leaving the school. Jack was hurt but alive and that made her heart sing, but part of her was mourning for Ameth. "What happened to Owen?" Emera asked.

They began to hear the chopper approaching. "Flares!" Canva called as several of the men lit green smoke flares to signal their location to the large helicopter as it made its approach.

"Canva!" Jack called. Canva gave a few more orders and then went to Jack. "What happened to the man that was lifted out?"

"You didn't hear?" Canva asked. They shook their heads. "He never made it to the hospital. Died shortly before they set it down."

Bridge from his position on the ground laughed. Jack and Emera turned toward the sound. The old soldier's eyes were opened, and he cackled until his voice cracked. Then, licking his lips, he said, "Old Lindstrom knows how to follow an order."

Jack fell on his knees beside the man. "What does that mean?" Jack repeated his question, shaking the man.

Canva put a hand on Jack's shoulder. "Ease up. He doesn't know what he's talking about."

"Hell I don't." Bridge screamed as the helicopter's engine hummed loudly, signaling that it was coming in for a landing. "Couldn't let the truth out. National security. He was a casualty of war."

Jack pulled the man up by his collar. "You killed him! You Bastard!" Jack yelled, trying to draw back with his wounded hand but the stitches and severity of the cuts prevented it.

Canva pulled Jack off of Bridge and pulled him aside. "Had to be done." Bridge cried. "Old Doc knew what to do."

Bridge quieted down and Canva looked directly at Jack. "If you try anything, I will have to shoot you. I cannot allow you to harm my superior."

"I don't need to." Jack said, staring past Canva.

Canva turned around and saw the black rubber handle and the black stainless steel blade that was buried deep into Bridge's chest. The man's face was caught between a look of anguish and amusement. Reaching behind him, Canva felt the empty sheath. It was his knife. Emera stood next to the body crying. Jack walked past Canva and put an arm around her. "It had to be done." Jack said.

Emera cried on his shoulder and nodded her head. The helicopter landed, and Jack and Emera walked up the ramp into the hold where canvas seats were bolted against the sides. The children followed with the soldiers bringing up the rear. Canva was the last one on; he spoke into a radio handset mounted on the wall near the rear hatch, and the helicopter lifted into the air. As the ramp started to close, Jack saw the back portion of the school engulfed in flames and the surrounding forest was aflame as well.

It was an hour helicopter ride. Jack drifted in and out of sleep, and then he felt the jostle as the helicopter set down on the hard surface of its landing pad. The ramp opened, and Jack saw the neat buildings, Humvees, and olive green trucks and knew they had reached their destination. Then, he saw something that set him on edge. There were several trucks parked outside of the landing area and a small group of MPs were approaching.

Epilogue

Jack sat on the small, hard cot and stared out the large Plexiglas plating that comprised one wall of his cell. The other three were concrete with a steel door lodged in the center of the rear. The glass showed a hallway and a small, windowed booth where guards would sit and watch and talk into radios. He assumed it was a control room. Currently, he was being held in an underground facility. He did not know how deep it went or how big it was. It had been three months since they landed on this base. Three months since Canva turned Jack, Emera, Ruby and all of the students over to the MPs. Canva had known that the survivors would not be let go, but he had kept silent and watched as the civilian survivors were taken prisoner. "I see you again, you're a dead man." Jack had told Canva as the metallic restraints had been placed on his wrists. Jack was almost completely recovered from the wounds he had received fighting Friedkin.

The fire that consumed the school and the town of Mead's Hall had not left any survivors in the area; at least, that was the story the news agencies were reporting. No doubt that was the story they were fed. Once a week, Jack was allowed to visit with Emera. She and the children from the school were being housed in a separate section of the facility. Her mane of black hair had been cut short to keep in line with military standards. The children were still being taught and were being fed decently. Jack was allowed, too, into what they called "the playground." It was in fact an outdoor obstacle course. The good thing was that Jack had been conditioning himself; he knew trouble was brewing. With his glass wall to the hallway, he saw the gurneys and the men on them begging for death. He heard the screams and when the lights would dim, there were times he could hear the faint sound of howling come through the vent.

He had seen at least a dozen different men wheeled by on the gurneys. There was no way to be certain how many were being held in the facility. One thing was certain, though: Friedkin had not been the only one. Some teams had captured their targets, and Jack knew that this prison they had built to study these monstrosities would not hold them forever. He only hoped he could find a way to get out with Emera, Ruby, and the rest before all hell broke loose.

THE END.

If you enjoyed Friedkin's Curse, then please leave a review at Amazon, Goodreads, or wherever you would like to. Your reviews are greatly appreciated and can make or break an independent author.

Other Works by Seth Tucker

The Winston & Baum Steampunk Adventures Series

Winston & Baum and the Secret of the Stone Circle - Winston & Baum are two men who are no strangers to danger, and the mythical creatures that plague the English countryside. Now Queen Victoria, a cyborg of brass and bolts, has charged them with an important mission. Representatives from the fairy world have warned that dark forces are gathering to conquer the British Isles and rid it of man and good fey alike. In an unholy bond between the dark races of the English fey and German monsters, a child has been ordered dead. If the girl dies, then the evil forces will be unstoppable. Traveling the English countryside in search of the child, led only by dreams, Winston & Baum must confront overwhelming odds to rescue the girl and keep her safe. The German forces are not willing to surrender so easily and it is discovered that everything is not as it seems. Winston & Baum will have to unravel the Secret of the Stone Circle to save God, Queen, and country.

Winston & Baum and the Seven Mummies of Sekhmet - Dan Winston & Lee Baum, two adventurers who hunt monsters for a living, find themselves pitted against unimaginable forces. Seven mummies have recently been discovered, the Priests of Sekhmet. On the unveiling of one of these mummies, a madman, with supernatural powers, steals the headdress of the priest. In their search for the thief, they discover a startling truth: when the headdresses of the seven priests are brought together, they have the power to awaken the sleeping goddess, Sekhmet. Now Dan, Lee, and their goblin assistant, Brackish, must travel to the sands of Egypt, where they will battle foes not seen in our world for centuries. In a race against time, Winston & Baum will have to stop a nearly invincible madman, prevent an ancient evil from being reawakened, and save the world from an age of darkness. Just another day on the job for the exterminators of the strange and weird.

E-shorts by Seth Tucker

Richard Rex & the Succubus of Whitechapel - A murder in Whitechapel is not uncommon, but the state of the body requires someone more adept at unusual crime than Scotland Yard. Richard Rex, agent of the Queen, must track down this supernatural killer. Can he find it before it claims more victims?

Terror Beneath Cactus Flats (A Weird Western) - Jed, the fresh faced deputy Marshall of Cactus Flats, finds himself put to the test as an unknown evil besieges the small town. In order to save the townsfolk, Jed will have to venture into the old abandoned mines and confront the evil awaiting within.

Friends Don't Let Friends be Undead - Three days after her husband dies, Lily is shocked to see him staring at her from outside her home. Calling on the four men he trusted most, Lily relies on them to place Steve back into his eternal rest. Guided by his journal, his friends will find that the man they loved has been replaced by a vicious fiend that will stop at nothing to sate its thirst for blood.

All titles available on Kindle

Author's Note

Friedkin's Curse actually started as a nightmare my wife had one night. Needless to say, the story was different from her nightmare after I got a hold of it. The longest story I had ever done prior to this was a twenty page short story. Friedkin's Curse decimated that record. Most of my friends asked me how I wrote this story and as I always say, I have no idea. It started out as a short story that just kept getting longer. I'm very excited that you chose to take the trip with me.

I hope you cherish the characters as much as I did, and I hope the adventure they have was as thrilling for you as it was for me.

Acknowledgements

The adventure that you have just went on owes a great deal of thanks to my wife, Caralyn, who read through this story first and gave me great ideas. Also, she never let me give up. My editor, Mac, did a great job going through and helping me to provide you with the best product possible. Lastly, I owe a very heartfelt thanks to you, the reader, without you this story would never find life in your imaginations. Thank you.

About the Author

Seth Tucker was born; it was then that his adventure began. He has traveled the world and seen great sites. At one time, he was even in the Sahara Desert with a chimp surrounded by silver backs. He began writing at an early age. Friedkin's Curse is his first novel. His three great loves are his wife, horror, and BACON. He is quite the elusive creature, many search parties have never returned while trying to find his lair. It is suspected that he resides near Atlanta. You can follow his misadventures and leave comments about the book at www.radioactiverabbitink.com.

Made in the USA
Lexington, KY
29 July 2018